The Boat

Wendy Newton-Fenbow was brought up in Cley-next-the-sea, on the North Norfolk coast. As a teacher she worked in schools in Chichester, Hillingdon, Notting Hill, King's Lynn and Terrington St Clements.

Wendy met her husband at the home of Hepzibah Menuhin, Yehudi's sister, where she attended International Seminars in Education. She lived with them for some time while teaching in London and nursed her husband for nine years. He died on a kidney machine in 1971, having recovered from cancer of the spine from which he suffered for some time, before and after they met.

Wendy now lives in Norwich.

The Boat

A Novel

Wendy Newton-Fenbow

ISBN 978-0-9955806-2-6

9 780995 580626

First published in paperback in Great Britain in 2016
by Wendy Newton-Fenbow

Front cover photo of Southwold harbour entrance
All photos by the author

A big thank you to Ruth Rudd for all her work in
preparing the layout, and to Steven Pyke of Page Bros
for the printing and binding – Wendy Newton-Fenbow

Printed and bound by Page Bros, Norwich Ltd

Dedicated to all my friends
everywhere

Chapter One

Southwold, a place of enchantment, with a history of fishing folk and families who came to the seaside. A beach of pebbles and sand and little beach huts, reminders of earlier times. The church stands majestically guarding the town, the white lighthouse, like a sentinel, doing likewise. This is a little paradise for the discerning, for walks in the morning quietness, for renewing the unquiet spirit. There was no quiet for Jill Marston, who sat on her garden seat clutching the left arm of the chair so tightly her knuckles became white. She and Bob, her husband, had felt uneasy since their daughter Susan brought home a new boyfriend for the weekend. This time was more difficult than usual as Susan had arrived home engaged to be married to Andrew Denby, whom they had not met before. They had not established the background of this man and felt unable to ask questions. Sensing a degree of tension, Susan said, 'Let's go for a walk along the beach, Andrew doesn't know Southwold,' Relieved, they agreed and all got up to put on coats or anoraks. Away from the shelter of the house the September breeze was chilly, the house was situated off Marlborough Road. The party slipped down onto the promenade south of the pier. Susan and Andrew walked hand in hand in front of Bob and Jill. After a short time they stopped and looked back, and the east wind blew across Susan's face.

'I like to see your hair hanging loose,' Andrew smiled, as she bought her long, dark, straight hair to one side and held it down with her free hand. Andrew glanced around, unused to seeing the vast amount of water stretching away to infinity in front of him. 'It's a small pier, has some been washed away?' Andrew asked as Jill and Bob caught up with them.

'Partly that, and partly taken away as a precaution against invasion during the last war,' Bob replied, gazing down at the pier in the far distance. They turned and walked down towards it, passing the jutting groynes that protect Southwold against erosion.

'The beach is crowded during the summer but now the children have gone back to school it's quieter, thank goodness,' Jill commented, now feeling a little more at ease.

'I don't suppose the shopkeepers and hotels feel that way. The town must be very quiet and isolated during the off season,' Andrew surmised. 'Except for the fishing industry and Adnam's brewery, and of course visitors come to eat in the good restaurants,' Bob said, boasting the advantages of his home town.

'And the occasional birdwatchers who turn up, especially in the Autumn and Spring' Susan told him.

Jill and Bob slowed down a little and were some way behind the young couple when Jill asked, 'What do you think of him, Darling?'

'He seems nice enough, too early to say really,' Bob replied.

'They haven't said when they intend to get married and I

don't like prying. I might be able to get her on her own with an opportunity to ask her,' Jill said, looking out to sea.

'As long as she's happy, we've got nothing to worry about,' Bob concluded.

'Well, it would be nicer for us if we got to like him,' Jill said, glancing at her husband.

'She's got her head screwed on OK,' Bob reassured his wife.

Andrew jumped off the wall of the promenade and Susan sat on it, dangling her legs, waiting for Andrew to help her down, when he pretended to pull her down onto the beach by her ankles. She screamed and he lifted her down, laughing.

'Young love!' Bob said and Jill smiled with him. Andrew and Susan ran to the water hand in hand and on reaching it Susan took off her socks and shoes and tiptoed into the foaming shoreline. The breakers rolled in and slapped her on the legs, Andrew laughed as she made a face.

'It's a bit cold at first,' she gasped, 'but you soon get used to it. Are you coming in?'

'No, thanks, I don't go for discomfort,' Andrew smiled.

'Typical city type,' Susan teased him, shuffling her feet through the water, trying to keep on the sandy parts and avoiding the pebbles. Bob and Jill climbed the steps between the beach huts and crossed the grass, leaving the lovebirds to themselves for a while, and returned home.

Jill was preparing dinner when Susan and Andrew returned.

'It's getting dark outside already,' Susan said as she entered the lounge where her father was sitting in the armchair drinking a beer.

'Adnams I assume!' said Andrew, following Susan in.

'But of course! Would you like one?' Bob asked him.

'I'd prefer a whisky at this time, if I may?' Andrew said.

'Certainly you may,' Bob assured him, hoping it might loosen Andrew's tongue a bit so they could relax more.

'Cheers, thanks,' Andrew said, raising the glass Bob handed to him.

'To you and Susan,' Bob said, lifting his glass to them, but feeling unsure of the choice his daughter had made for a husband. Susan excused herself and went to change before dinner, she came back looking tidy in a crisp pale blue shirt and black skirt.

'Oh, you've changed, have you? I'd better go and put on a clean shirt' Andrew said, looking her up and down.

'You don't have to,' Bob said, being polite. Andrew put down his glass and went upstairs.

'Well honey, when are you getting married?' Bob asked Susan, without wasting any more time to find out.

'Next year sometime. Andrew doesn't know if he can get Christmas off and I want to spend it with you both, and Robert, if he can get home then,' Susan informed him.

'Good, he is coming home, all being well,' Bob said.

'Marvellous! When did you hear?'

'Last week. We didn't want to say anything until we knew what you were doing,' he explained, looking with affection at his daughter.

'What fun, my brother is coming home for Christmas! I would like you to come home then, Andrew,' she told him as he came back through the door.

'I'm not sure if I shall have the time off yet, but that sounds nice. Am I invited?' He smiled, turning to Bob.

'Of course, Old Boy!' Bob said, 'Especially if it means we can have our Girl home with us,' he smiled. Bob thought this would be a good time to ask Andrew what his work was specifically, but at that moment Jill came in to say dinner was nearly ready.

Susan jumped up and put her arm round her mother's shoulder. 'Oh, I'm so sorry, I should have been in there helping you,' she confessed, 'Can I do anything to help or is it too late?' she asked.

'It's all right, you can fill the dishwasher afterwards,' Jill smiled.

They went into the dining room and Andrew was given the seat where Robert normally sat, opposite Susan.

'Mmm, smells lovely,' Andrew said politely. The meal was passed in polite small-talk and discussing what they would do the next day, Sunday. It was decided they would go for a drive, show Andrew the coastline northwards as far as Lowestoft.

'We can have lunch at the Sparrows' Nest and visit the Maritime museum there,' suggested Bob, he continued, 'There is a magnificent display of model fishing boats and wherries like those used in the past in this area of the coast.'

'Yes,' agreed Jill, 'and the Sparrows' Nest was used during the last war by the Royal Navy Patrol. They had offices there. I remember being told that Lord Haw-Haw broadcast over the wireless during the war when I was a child. He used to say "the Germans are coming tonight, to drop eggs on your Sparrows' Nest", meaning of course bombs. But they never did succeed, although they tried!' they all smiled.

During the evening Bob and Jill established that Andrew worked in some capacity with the Port of London Authority. He did not volunteer more than that. Susan only added that he was 'quite high up', implying that Andrew was being modest in saying little.

Whatever that means, Jill thought. She supposed that Susan would enlighten them in due course, so shook the worry from her mind, of her daughter's future in financial terms, when she was married. Jill had made the bed up in Robert's room. In her old fashioned way she did not expect Susan and Andrew to sleep together. Susan had not mentioned the matter to her Mother on their arrival, and was glad that Jill had made her own decision without the embarrassment it would have caused her. Even so it irritated her little. *She must know we sleep together in London,* Susan thought.

However, some time after they had all gone to bed and the house was quiet, Susan crept along the landing and gently opened Andrew's door. He shot up in bed and was about to speak but Susan put her finger to her lips and silently closed the door. He moved over as far as possible in a single bed and she eased herself in beside him.

'I wanted to come to you but I didn't know which floorboards creek,' Andrew whispered. They suppressed their mirth.

Andrew lifted her nighty and stroked her smooth, silky body, at the same time kissing her mouth and breasts. She pulled him to her and they melted into one rhythmical ecstasy. They then lay entwined for some time, caressing each other and whispering in loving contentment.

'I'll slip back quietly now and go to the bathroom en route.

If either of them are awake they'll think one of us is going to the loo,' Susan smiled. She slid out of the bed and as Andrew blew her a kiss he turned on his back and, forgetting the size of the bed, disappeared with a thump onto the floor on the other side. Susan forget to stay quiet and bending over, holding her stomach, exploded into giggles as she ran around to help him up.

'Shush, they'll hear you,' Andrew said, climbing back into bed.

'They'll have heard the thump, enough to shake the whole house,' Susan tried to whisper while laughing. She kissed him on the forehead while he rubbed his arm and then his buttock.

'Kiss it and make it better!' he told her.

'No way, I'm off. Sleep well,' Susan said still smiling broadly. She blew him a kiss as she glanced back at him before closing the door quietly. Her heart pounded as she tiptoed to the bathroom and then back to her bedroom.

'Something's going on out there, listen!' Bob said as he and Jill lay exhausted in each other's arms after making love. 'They sound as though they've been doing the same as us.'

'Darling, don't be crude, I'd rather not think about it,' Jill said, unable to do anything else. She lay there worrying again. 'It would be awful if she became pregnant and they broke off the engagement,' she said, looking into Bob's face.

'Stop worrying and go to sleep, she's old enough to look after herself. She's not a child any more,' Bob said, wishing she was and that they could turn the clock back.

'These days young people seem to snatch whatever joy they can. They don't have to get in the family way though. There are enough precautions if they take responsibility for themselves,' Jill reasoned aloud.

Bob was breathing heavily and Jill wondered for how long she had been talking to herself. She turned away from him and after what seemed and interminable time she fell asleep. Susan lay awake for some time. She thought of how her parents would make a fuss of their grandchildren when she and Andrew had babies. She dropped off to sleep with a contented smile on her face.

After a pleasant Sunday, Susan and Andrew thanked her parents for the nice weekend, and drove back to London.

'I've come to like him, haven't you?' Jill said, looking at Bob.

'He's all right,' Bob commented grudgingly. He felt a sudden pang of jealousy in seeing his daughter going off with another man. He realised his little girl had flown the nest and grown up into an independent woman.

'I expect they'll soon be back for another weekend,' Jill said, sensing his thoughts, which she secretly shared.

'I hope so,' Bob said quietly.

'At least she's almost certain to come home for Christmas,' Jill went on.

'Before that, I hope,' Bob forced a smile and squeezed his wife's hand as they made their way back into the house.

Chapter Two

The next time Andrew and Susan visited her parents for the weekend Andrew took them out to dinner on the Saturday evening. He expressed the wish to see the harbour and fishing boats, so they planned to do that the next day. Jill suggested they went to church and they all complied. Susan wanted Andrew to see inside the interesting building and to hear the fifteenth-century wooden soldier of the War of the Roses which strikes a bell before the service starts.

'It's called "Jack of the Clock", but more interesting is the medieval screen showing paintings of the Apostles,' Bob informed Andrew.

On entering St Edmund's the next day, Andrew was impressed at how light the whole church was inside. Susan whispered to him that some of the windows had been blown out by bombs in the war and replaced with plain glass. After the service they walked back to the house in the midday sun. Later Susan and Andrew left to explore the harbour. Jill and Bob did not go as the October day had become blustery. Susan drove so that Andrew could look about him and because she knew the way, as they drove through the town Susan pointed out the interesting buildings and landmarks.

'What a pretty place, and so many grassy areas,' Andrew observed.

'Oh yes! The town was badly damaged by fire, in 1600-and-something, I think 1659. It was rebuilt with small greens in between houses to prevent such colossal damage happening again,' Susan explained.

'I wonder other towns haven't had the sense to do likewise,' Andrew said.

'Probably some have,' Susan said. They came to the Common, and Susan drove down to it, past the Water Tower, down the hill, on past the golf course and turned past the house on the corner. They drove on past the Marine Services Building and as near as they could get to the long bridge that crosses the River Blyth to Walberswick. On the left of them a number of small black huts looked sad with little white flags on some of them as if they were trying to keep up appearances.

'What a lot of various sized boats there are here,' Andrew observed.

'The fisherman can get out of the harbour in small boats at any time. They know the channel. The bigger ones have to wait for the high tide,' Susan explained, 'The harbour isn't that easy to navigate, the sandbanks are changing all the time,' she went on.

'You seem to be very knowledgeable on the subject!' Andrew said, smiling.

'I was born here, and used to sail in my youth,' Susan laughed, 'Let's get out and walk.'

Hand in hand they walked to the middle of the footbridge where Andrew studied the banks on both sides.

'Is there a coastguard here?' he asked

'I don't think there is one between Cromer on the north Norfolk coast and Walton on the Naze, further south from here,' Susan informed him.

'That's a great distance, but I suppose they use helicopters and radar now to guard the coast,' Andrew said. The subject was dropped. Andrew became thoughtful and quiet.

'Are you OK? You've stopped asking questions!' Susan said jokingly.

'Oh yes, I thought it would be nice to have a yacht here sometime.'

'It would cost the earth and then you have the mooring and the upkeep of it each year.' Susan warned him.

'All the same, I'll think about it,' he said. As they walked across the rest of the bridge, Susan told Andrew about the Ghost of the Ferry Boatman, whom some of the people have supposedly seen on the south side of the River Blyth where they were heading. 'Then I'm glad it's daylight!' Andrew said.

'Some ghosts walk by day,' she informed him.

'Or float past you like this!' Andrew pretended to be a ghost.

'I love you, my future husband,' Susan laughed, putting her arm around his waist. Andrew thought the small huts on stilts were rather fun.

'More sand and less mud here,' Andrew said.

'In the 17th century the French and English fleets fought off the Dutch, in Sole Bay, offshore here. It was a hard battle and many bodies were washed up along this shore.'

'What a ghastly sight that must have been,' Andrew said, frowning.

'In the 18th century the six cannons standing on Gun Hill were put there to defend Southwold. I'll show you on the way home,' Susan said.

They walked briskly in the cool wind, only stopping to kiss or look at the pretty houses and gardens of Walberswick. Then they ran back across the bridge to keep warm.

Back at the car they sat and cuddled for ten minutes with the engine running to get the car warm inside.

'We can see the cannons another day, if you don't mind?' Susan said.

They drove home. When they arrived at the front door Jill opened it looking upset.

'What's wrong Mum?' Susan asked, her tummy turning over.

'Robert has rung. He can't get home for Christmas after all. He's coming in November instead,' Jill explained. Susan was relieved it was nothing worse than that.

'Oh well! At least we'll see him soon. We can have a little celebration then and exchange presents and enjoy ourselves just as much while he's here,' Susan said, drawing breath.

'Yes of course,' Jill agreed, 'But it won't be quite the same,' she added as they went in and shut out the cold.

The family spent the evening discussing plans for Robert's homecoming and watching television. Andrew and Susan decided to drive back to London after dinner. They travelled down the A12 and off it to Susan's flat in Walthamstow. Andrew decided to stay the night with her as he was tired, having driven all the way. Susan made coffee while he went to have a quick shower. He returned in Susan's towelling dressing gown. She laughed.

'You look like a white stork, with your long legs and knobbly knees,' she said, pronouncing her K as she had learned in German.

'I come to bring you baby,' he said, in a German accent.

'A little premature Darling, time enough when we are married,' Susan smiled, handing Andrew his mug. She turned the fire up further and they caressed each other's bodies between sips of hot milky coffee. His tiredness had left him. He took her shoulders and gently brought them to rest on the lamb's wool rug they were on. He undid her blouse, her bra and the gently pulled off the rest of her clothes. She waited eagerly for him to throw off his dressing gown. She pulled him to her as he bent towards her. He leaned on his elbows and looked into her eyes as they made love in the warmth of her lounge.

Andrew left early for work the next morning. Susan got ready to go to the bank in the city where she worked. She managed to get permission to have the Friday and Monday off so that she would be in Southwold when her brother came home in mid-November. She hoped Andrew would get off sometime that weekend so that he could meet Robert. During the evening Susan rang Andrew to tell him the good news but he was non-committal, telling her that he did not know whether or not he could get away. She put the phone down feeling rather deflated. He usually managed to be free at weekends and she wondered if there was something wrong at work. It seemed too early for a pre-Christmas rush at the Port. *Perhaps some colleagues are still taking late holidays*, Susan thought. She busied herself tidying the flat for the rest of the evening to give herself something else to think about. In fact, Susan saw less of

Andrew than previously and his excuse was that he had to work overtime, as she had suspected. She saw him the week before Robert's homecoming when one evening he arrived at her flat looking tired and fraught.

'Why are you so busy these days? You look worn out,' Susan said.

'I'm all right, just a lot more work on, that's all,' he said, not looking at her. He sat down wearily and rubbed his face. Susan began to worry that he might be ill in some way. She said nothing but went to the kitchen to prepare dinner for them. Andrew got up and poured himself a glass of whisky. He called to her to ask if she wanted a drink, she peered around the door.

'I'll have the same as you, please, with some soda in it,' she said, seeing his neat whisky in his hand. He poured it out and took it to her. She kissed him and he returned to his chair. Not much was said before or after the meal. Saddened by the unusual atmosphere Susan felt depressed. She cleared the table and went to where he was sitting.

'Darling, there is something wrong, isn't there? Why don't you tell me?' Andrew forced a smile and made an effort to brighten up.

'No, my Love, I'm just overtired, that's all. I'll be all right after a good night's sleep,' he again forced a smile.

Not long after, Andrew got up to leave. Susan wanted him to stay the night as he'd had a drink, as well as being tired.

'It's all right, I've had some coffee since then. I'd better get back to Chigwell, it isn't that far and it isn't that late' he decided. 'It's better than getting you up earlier than necessary.' Susan did not think it wise to argue that the alcohol was still in his blood, despite the coffee. She went to the door with him and they kissed.

'Goodnight Darling, take care and phone me when you get back home so I don't worry. Please!' she added, seeing a slight look of irritation on his face. She closed the door quietly when she heard him open the outside door and leave.

Susan busied herself washing up while waiting for Andrew to phone. She felt troubled by his sudden tiredness and still concerned about his indecision on the visit to meet Robert which played on her mind a little. She went to bed but took a long time to get to sleep, possibilities kept passing through her mind, repeating themselves over and over again. The thought that disturbed her the most was the possibility that he had found another woman, and was finding difficulty in breaking the news to her. The idea was devastating enough at that time of night, when any worry, however small, becomes blown up out of all proportion. She was determined to ask Andrew the next day. When daylight came and Susan was preparing for work she felt she could see things in their proper perspective. She smiled to herself for thinking that Andrew could deceive her by having a relationship with someone else. She went off to work in a more relaxed state of mind.

Andrew did not ring that evening and Susan went out to meet a friend. She had neglected her girl-friends since becoming involved with Andrew, and felt glad to have the chance to be independent for a change. Three days passed before she tried to contact him. She expected he had rung her and found that she was out the previous evenings, though he'd left no message. She rang a number of times but could not get hold of him.

At last, the following afternoon after work Susan went to the café in the city and bought herself a tea and a cream cake. She suddenly felt lonely and rang Andrew's office number from her mobile before going home.

'Hello Darling, what's troubling you that you ring me at work?' he asked, sounding quite happy, as if he was unaware of the rift that Susan felt.

'I wondered how you were, I tried to ring you last night but you were out,' she felt silly making such a remark, as if he didn't know.

'Yes, so were you,' he laughed, 'I tried to ring you the night before last, I didn't leave a message, where were you?'

'I was with June for the evening,' Susan told him, relieved that at least he had tried to contact her.

Men don't worry about trivialities like women do. She thought, *women possess too much intuition and are more sensitive to atmosphere than men.*

'When can you come over?' She asked, tentatively.

'I'll be there some point during the weekend, I'm not sure exactly when, but I'll ring you before then. I must go and get on now. Bye darling, take care of yourself.' He rang off before Susan could say anything more. She stood looking at the phone before pressing the off button, and was almost crying. She realised someone was watching her and put the phone in her pocket.

Susan made her way to the underground, wondering why Andrew had been so abrupt and indecisive. She walked with her head down, in miserable despair. Her woman's intuition was working overtime again and she began to think all her fears were justified. Andrew had never been anything but attentive and warm before, even on the phone. The phone rang just as she was putting her key in the lock of her door of her flat, she ran to answer it, her heart full of anticipation.

'Hello my love, how are you?' it was her mother, and for the moment Susan could not control her emotions enough to reply.

'Darling, are you all right? You sound puffed, nothing wrong is there?'

'Hello Mum, no I've just this minute got in,' Susan answered with a false smile she was glad her mother couldn't see.

'Darling, you are coming home next weekend aren't you? We're picking Robert up from Paddington Station on Thursday afternoon,' Jill told her excitedly.

'Oh yes, I've managed to get time off from Thursday evening, till the following Tuesday. How long is Robert staying?, I'm longing to see him, I'll follow you up in my own car so that I can get back on Monday night.'

'I don't know how long he's staying, I imagine a week. I didn't like to ask him before he even gets here. Won't Andrew be able to come along with you then? Robert is looking forward to meeting your fiancé, my love.' Jill said. Susan assured her that Andrew would join them if he was able, if only to put her mother's mind at rest. She was not at all sure herself what his movements were.

Chapter Three

It turned out that Andrew was able to join the Marston family during the weekend that Robert was home, but only for a short time. In fact, he drove up early on the Sunday to partake in the little celebration Jill and Bob put together for their son in lieu of Christmas. Andrew's intentions were to return to London in the late evening. This plan suited Jill as Robert was able to keep his own room and none of the family were put out, except Susan of course. She was not at all happy when Andrew rang her on the Wednesday before she went to Suffolk, to tell her he could not spend the entire weekend there.

'What are you up to that you can't get off at the weekends these days? Have you got another woman?' She asked hotly, her great disappointment causing her anger to well up within her so that she no longer stopped to consider that she should hold back.

'No Darling, of course I haven't, believe me, I love you, and you only!' Andrew said, horrified at her suspicions.

'Then why can't you come up earlier? Why are you always too busy to be with me these days? I hardly ever see you. Is it going to be like this when we are married? If so, it's not going to be much of a life for either of us,' Susan went on at a pace before Andrew could interrupt her.

'Susan, Love, I have to work hard at present. I want to give you all you deserve; to provide you with the sort of life you have been used to, a nice house and all that goes with it.' Andrew reasoned with her.

'I want to be with you Andrew, anywhere. That's more important to me than a big house and luxuries. Anything we want we can work for together and buy them as we can afford them,' Susan began to feel bad that she had raved at him and her frustration ebbed from her as she realised Andrew's reasons for working overtime. She resented that she had mentioned her suspicions in thinking he had another woman, a niggling thought that she had managed to suppress until then.

Now the weekend was here and Susan was enjoying her day with her brother and Andrew. They seemed to be getting on fine together. Andrew was happy in the family environment, having no family of his own since his parents were killed in a car crash and his guardian aunt had followed his grandparents to the grave when Andrew was in his late teens. He had lived for a short time in the YMCA hostel and eventually moved into the flat which he now lived.

After lunch the three young ones walked along the shore, Susan between the two men, sometimes linking arms with them both, their hands in their pockets to keep warm against the chill November breeze.

'It's great to be home again and to smell the sea air' Robert said, breathing in deeply.

'No paddling today,' Susan smiled at Andrew.

'I might throw you in!' he laughed, grabbing her arm. She pulled away and ran against the wind, her hair blowing out behind her. Andrew caught up and wrapped his arms around her tightly, pretending to pull her towards the water. She screamed to her brother for help. Andrew then swung her round to face him and kissed her on the cheek till their mouths met in a long embrace.

Robert smiled to himself, glad that his sister was so happy. He looked away and searched for shells among the sand and shingle. These he would keep and take away with him to remind him of home and especially of that precious moment. He loved the sea as much as Susan did and stood for some time watching the waves folding towards the shore. They crashed onto the beach at his feet as if exhausted by their journey, then drew the sand and pebbles in foaming streaks to join them, back into the depths again, *like the cycle of life itself,* Robert thought.

He wandered along and caught up with the loving couple, who by that time, had relinquished their embrace and were waiting for him to catch up with them. They continued along the beach, keeping close to the shore. A mother and small son were coming towards them. She looked down, picking up shells and tiny stones that glistened wet. The boy put his foot in the foamy ridge of the waterline, wetting his shoe. He looked towards his mother who had not noticed. This encouraged him to do the same again.

Little demon, thought Susan, as they came towards him. He stepped further into the trickle which washed over both his feet. Intent on what he was doing none of the grown-ups noticed in time the gigantic wave crash down offshore. It swept towards the beach and threw the small child to the ground. It pulled him into its strong arms of foaming wrath. Susan screamed as they ran to his aid. His mother was by this time up to her waist in the water trying to grab him. In panic she screamed for help. Andrew threw off his anorak, then his shoes, as he ran, and was in the water. He swam to where he thought the boy was.

'There!' yelled Robert as loud as he could against the roar of the sea and the screaming child's mother. Andrew glanced to where he was pointing. He saw the boy surface, not far from him. He reached out and grabbed his leg. Treading water Andrew turned him face upwards. At that moment they were both swept sideways with the current and tossed over the incoming waves. They vanished from view.

Susan and Robert ran to where they were. They went into the raging sea as far as they dared and saw Andrew desperately trying to reach the shore again. He was gripping the boy with one hand and paddling with the other. Robert pulled off his jacket and holding it by a sleeve lashed the rest out as far as he could for Andrew to catch. Susan gripped his free hand and wrist to prevent him from being swept off his feet and joining the other two.

The next wave lifted Andrew and the boy high and pounded them onto the shore near enough for Robert to yell to Andrew to catch the sleeve. At the second attempt Andrew succeeded and was pulled down with the boy on top of him. Robert grabbed his arm and held him there till the next wave had washed over them and ebbed away. Susan gripped the child by his anorak while Robert helped Andrew to drag himself onto dry land. He sank exhausted and shivering onto the sand.

Robert took the boy from Susan and laid him on his back. He began to give him resuscitation while his mother had hysterics at seeing her son unconscious at her feet. Susan covered Andrew with her jacket although she felt cold enough. She rubbed his arms and legs to get some feeling into them again. They were all shivering, partly from shock and partly from the bitterly cold water. Susan then jumped up and looked frantically over the beach to see if anyone was about, but saw no one. Their mobile phones had been ruined by the sea. She called to Robert that she would run to a phone for help. Looking down at Andrew huddled under her jacket red with cold, she said, 'I'll be as quick as I can, Darling, you were very brave,' and she raced as fast as she was able across the sand, glad to get a little warmer in doing so. On terra firma she ran faster to the phone box. Out of breath and trying to sound as calm as she could manage with the vision of the trauma in her mind she dialled 999 and asked for an ambulance. It took longer than she imagined, having been asked her name, the exact position of the party, number and problem. She then rang her parents to tell them to come to the beach in the car as fast as they could. The urgency of her voice, on the verge of tears, told them not to ask questions but to move themselves quickly.

Robert, in the meantime, was almost giving up hope of saving the boy but persevered by gently breathing into his lungs while alternately compressing with two fingers, his small chest. He longed for the ambulance to come and take over with their specialist equipment. The mother squatted at his side, sobbing. With difficulty Andrew got to his feet and joined them to give his support. Suddenly Robert gave a grunting exclamation which was all he was able to impart when he saw the boys chest rise and fall of its own accord. He felt the pulse in the child's upper arm and with a look of triumph and tears rolling down his cheeks he sat back on his heels and smiled broadly at the mother and Andrew. She crawled to her son's side, and pulled him to her, this time crying for joy.

'Let's lay him on his side till the ambulance comes, so that he doesn't choke,' Robert said, gently lifting him from the bosom of his mother. They surrounded him to keep the cold wind away from him and themselves as much as possible. The child's mother watched him from her tear-stained face and forced a smile of thanks.

'Well done old chap!' Andrew said, patting Robert on the back.

'I should be saying that to you,' Robert smiled, as Susan was seen running down the beach. She collapsed at their side. She hardly dared to look at the boy in case he was dead, but knew he wasn't as soon as she saw their faces. The boy's mother lifted herself up and fell into Susan's arms. They both wept for joy as the child moved and then opened his eyes to see everyone smiling at him through their tears. They saw the ambulance arrive above the promenade and two men soon joined them with equipment and a stretcher. They were as relieved as the rest to find the little boy alive and lifted him onto the stretcher wrapped in a thick blanket. By this time Andrew was shaking violently with hypothermia and the others were almost as cold.

'You'd better join us, Sir, for the night. You are in no state to go home like that,' one of the men advised.

'Oh, I'll be OK,' Andrew just managed to chatter through his teeth.

'You'd better go for tonight Andrew, to make sure,' Susan advised. 'Oh! Here come Mummy and Dad, thank goodness, but I wish I'd asked them to bring coats and rugs,' she said, waving to them as they came hurrying down the beach looking very worried, having seen the ambulance.

'Don't worry yourself, Madam, all will be well when we get these to the hospital,' one of the paramedics tried to reassure them.

'What's happened?' Jill asked, as they made their way hurriedly to the ambulance, but no one was in a condition to speak. Andrew suddenly fell to the ground, unable to make it to the parade, even with Susan's support. Robert knelt to help him. Susan was, by this time, crying with sheer release of tension and exhaustion. Her mother put her arms around Susan's shoulders while Bob ran to get rugs out of the car. They stayed beside Andrew and Robert till the ambulance men came with the stretcher and lifted Andrew onto it.

'Get the other two home as soon as possible and give them some warm sweet tea and a warm, not hot, bath. If they suffer from too much hypothermia ring the hospital,' The men advised as they closed the ambulance door and sped off. The party were silent as Bob drove them home. They asked no questions. Susan was quietly sobbing and both she and Robert were shivering with cold. Although the entire event had taken but twenty minutes it seemed to them like a lifetime.

'Sorry about the wet seats Dad,' Robert apologised through the chattering teeth as they heaved themselves out of the car.

'Don't worry about that my Boy,' his father said, 'thank goodness you are both all right. That's all that matters.'

Their son and daughter were helped indoors and upstairs to get out of their wet clothes and into the baths, glad to be in the warm at last. Jill took up the tea to Susan while she sat in the warm water getting the feeling back into her body. She had stopped crying and was thinking of the trauma that had taken place on the beach and wondering how Andrew was. Jill then went into the other bathroom with Roberts's tea and took away his wet clothes to put in the washing machine. The wet anoraks Bob hung up in the garage to dry, ready to take to the cleaners the next day.

When they were all together again by the log fire, the colour back in Robert's and Susan's cheeks, they told of all that had happened on the beach. Jill and Bob were full of admiration for all three of them, especially Andrew's bravery, and how they had all helped in saving the little boy's life.

'How marvellous that you were there, otherwise he would have surely drowned,' Jill said.

After their meal Susan rang the hospital to see how Andrew was and to ask about the boy and his mother. She heard that all was well. The mother and child and Andrew had been transferred to the James Paget hospital in Gorleston as the Southwold hospital had recently closed. Andrew was asleep so she could not talk to him but popped down with his clothes and some fruit and left a message to say that she would ring early the next morning. Robert and Susan then went to bed, both utterly exhausted. Robert slept soundly till the morning but Susan slept fitfully all night, it seemed to her, and had strange dreams of running away from things. She was awakened by her mother at 9am the next morning. Before breakfast she telephoned the James Paget Hospital to learn to her total amazement that Andrew had already left and insisted in going back to work.

'… against the doctor's advice, Miss Marston,' the Sister informed Susan emphatically.

Bob and Jill were equally surprised at hearing the news when Susan walked into the dining room, where they were halfway through breakfast, and told them. She felt very despondent that Andrew had not communicated with them before returning to London.

'Perhaps he thought it was it was too early to ring before he left', Susan said miserably, 'I'll ring him later at work, perhaps, though he doesn't like me to do that, normally.'

'He must be a very conscientious worker,' Jill commented.

'Don't worry Darling, I expect he'll contact you before the day is out,' Bob said, trying to comfort her.

Robert wandered into the dining room in his dressing gown, looking half asleep still, as the others were finishing their breakfast. Susan told him of the news from the hospital.

'I'm glad the kid and his mum are OK. I don't envy Andrew,' Robert said, seating himself down heavily at the table. The others waited for him to continue. He shook his head in disbelief.

'Business must be pressing. What does he actually do Sue?'

'Something to do with the import side, at the Port of London. I don't know what.'

'Surely nothing so important that he is forced to rush off like that,' Robert reasoned. Susan wished he would drop the subject and eat his breakfast, but he went on, 'Going back to work so soon. I think he ought to have rested here for a day or two. I feel lousy, tired and achy. I think I've got a cold coming' Robert commented, leaning back on his chair and rubbing his face with both hands.

'I hope not, eat some hot food. I've got some eggs and bacon in the oven,' Jill said, leaving the dining room to fetch them. Susan poured her brother some coffee and sat down in her chair opposite.

'I can't think why he had to rush off so soon. He could have rung the Port to say he wasn't well and told them what happened. I'm sure they would have understood,' Susan said looking at Robert.

'He's probably feeling OK after a good night's sleep. He seems a tough guy. Don't worry love. You rest today. I'm glad you have some time off while I'm home,' Robert smiled at his sister.

'You look as if you need some rest too, it's a good thing you don't have to go back for a week, you look awful,' Susan emphasized.

'Thanks, that makes me feel fine,' Robert said sarcastically.

Jill entered with Robert's breakfast and sat down at the table while he ate it, glad to have her two children with her.

Bob put down the newspaper the had been reading and pushed his chair back.

'I'll just pop down with the anoraks to the cleaners, they're beginning to smell a bit' he said, standing up.

'Get me some milk while you're there Darling,' his wife said as he was leaving the room.

'And some humbugs for me,' Robert called.

'And some chocies for me please!' Susan laughed, cheering up a little.

'The kids are home!' Bob commented as he went out the house.

'Good old Dad' Robert said between sips of coffee.

'You look a bit better now, but I'd stay in today and get some rest. The weather isn't very bright and it's not warm, the wind is easterly,' Jill told them.

'I'd like to get in the car later, perhaps after lunch, and go see the little boy and his mother in hospital' Susan told her mother.

'See how you feel when the time comes,' Jill said, clearing the breakfast things away.

'I don't think I will go with you. I'll wait and see how I fell tomorrow, I don't want to give the child a cold,' Robert said, 'if he hasn't got one already,' he added. 'By the way, what's his name? I forgot to ask.'

'It's Johnny, and his mother is called Alice. I think the nurse said their surname was Harris or Harrison. I rang and asked after the little lad who had nearly drowned' Susan told him.

'Well don't suppose there were too many of them, so you probably got the right one,' Robert teased her.

'If it hadn't been for you there would not have been even one' Susan said admiringly.

'A joint effort, I would say' he said.

The rest of the day Susan and her brother had together was spent telling each other how they were leading their lives and catching up on events that had passed since they had last seen each other. Susan went to the hospital and spent an hour with Johnny and his mother. She was overcome with gratitude for the risks the three of them had taken to save her son's life, and at the same time was still suffering from shock to some degree.

'I blame myself,' she told Susan miserably, 'I shouldn't have taken my eyes off him'

'You mustn't blame yourself, it all happened so quickly, don't worry about it. He's here, that's all that matters' Susan comforted her. A nurse came in with a cup of tea for Alice and a glass of orange juice for Johnny.

'Would you like a cup?' She asked Susan.

'No, thank you, I must go' Susan smiled at her, 'When will Mrs Harris and Johnny be able to go home?' she asked the nurse.

'Mrs Harrison' the nurse corrected Susan, 'will be able to go when the doctor says so, probably tomorrow, but I really can't say' she said, leaving the ward.

'I hope everything goes well for you now', Susan said, 'could I have your address and keep in touch?' she asked Alice.

'Of course, I live in Southwold. Just Johnny and me. I haven't got a husband. He walked out on me when Johnny was two. He's five now,' Alice said, looking at Johnny who was asleep on top of his bed in the small ward. She gave Susan her address and Susan laid a little bear she had bought on her way to the hospital on the pillow beside Johnny.

'Try and get some sleep yourself tonight and don't worry' Susan told her.

'Thanks a million, and thank those two brave men for me, please' Alice said, looking tenderly at Susan.

'I will,' Susan called back as she entered the corridor from the children's ward. She had not had the heart to tell Alice that one of those men was her fiancé. Alice had looked sad enough when she told Susan she was alone. As it was Susan felt a sudden pang of sadness herself on remembering that Andrew had left the hospital without letting her know. She had half a mind to ring his office while she was on her own before leaving the hospital but put the thought out of her mind. She had not the courage to so in case it was inconvenient. Andrew would be abrupt and that would make her more miserable than she already was. She stuffed her hands deep down into her mac pockets and made her way back to her car. *Elusive Andrew, are you always going to slip in and out of my life like this, without communicating, I wonder?* she thought.

Chapter Four

*A*ndrew had felt tired when he left the hospital on that Monday morning. He had to get down to Southwold harbour by seven in order to meet Reggie. He'd rung him from the hospital the night before and told Reggie he was in the area and would like to look at the boat. The hospital houseman was reluctant to discharge but Andrew put up a good front, though his common sense told him the doctor was right. He walked down to the river before light so as not to be seen and found Reggie waiting for him not far from the Marine shop.

'Hi! How do you feel? What the hell were you doing in there last night?' Reggie asked. He was most impressed when Andrew gave him a brief run-down of events.

'Well, well!' He said, 'This future brother in law of yours seems to have as much spunk as you. You must be a bloody good swimmer to conquer the sea at this time of year. Hellish cold too I should say. I can't swim far. For all my sailing experience I don't like getting wet!'

'I hope you never have to,' Andrew smiled.

'We'll leave the van here and go over to have a look at the vessel. She's moored over there.' Reggie pointed further up the creek. They walked briskly. The air was fresh at that time of the morning and Andrew felt cold inside.

'I'll have to ring the Port to say I'll be back this afternoon' Andrew informed Reggie.

'Christ! I thought we might be able to go out for an hour or two to give you a run in her' Reggie exclaimed, surprised.

'I can't today. Anyway, I'm not feeling too fit after yesterday's do'

'How soon can you manage to get back? I've got someone else interested in looking at her' Reggie lied.

'Can you be here on Thursday? I can get the morning off at least' Andrew told him.

'Yeah, if you can make it earlier, let me know' Reggie said, frowning.

As they walked along the river path Andrew wandered which of the boats moored to the bank ahead was the one he wanted to buy. Some were well kept and luxurious and some looked as if they had seen better days.

Reggie suddenly stopped next to a forty five footer that certainly looked as if it had retired long since. Andrew looked at Reggie to see if he was eyeing another next to it which appeared in better health. To his dismay, Reggie smiled and said,

'Here we are. This is it, old *Maggie,*' he said.

'Old is the operative word' Andrew told him, 'she doesn't look too seaworthy' he added, greatly disappointed.

'Oh, she's seaworthy alright. She only needs a coat of paint. Structurally she's quite OK,' Reggie said, hoping he could convince a Londoner with perhaps little knowledge of seafaring.

'When did you use her last?' Andrew asked, wondering if Reggie could remember.

'Quite recently' Reggie lied again.

'Come on board, have a look around her' he suggested, changing the conversation. Andrew followed him onto the deck and round the rail back to the stern. Reggie opened the hatch and descended the steps, taking a torch out of his pocket to see where he was going. He turned the light to the top of the steps to guide Andrew down.

'There's plenty of room down here, you see. When the old engine is going it generates the lights,' he said, trying to impress Andrew.

'The galley is here, and the bunks further up the bow. Come on.' Reggie encouraged Andrew. He followed, taking in as much as he could in what light there was. His impression was that the whole place needed cleaning up and giving a coat of paint.

'I'll bring my friend over to see it on Thursday,' Andrew told him, 'He and I are in partnership on this. If he thinks it's fit to take out to sea we'll go for a trip, if not we'll have to look elsewhere.'

'Fair enough' Reggie replied, not too pleased. He had hoped to clinch the deal that day.

'You'll come with us on the trial run, of course?' Andrew suggested, looking at Reggie.

'Yeah, OK,' he paused, then said, with a snarling smile, 'I thought you could manage a boat?!'

They stepped ashore. Andrew felt uneasy, and wasn't sure if he trusted or even liked this man.

'I've sailed a boat before, but my friend is more used to the fishing boats' Andrew was relying on the confidence Harry had shown when they discussed the issue. The two men shook hands after agreeing to go for a trip on the coming Thursday at about 3 o'clock when the tide would be up. They walked back to Reggie's van, Andrew suddenly realised he had no car, having come up to Susan's family by train.

'Could you give me a lift to the nearest phone box, I have to call a taxi, I haven't got my car here.' Andrew explained

'Where do you want to get to?' Reggie asked, puzzled.

'To Halesworth Station,' Andrew told him.

'I'll run you there for a fiver,' Reggie suggested, always on the make. Andrew thought this was a bit expensive but was glad to accept the offer. He had become suddenly tired and though the van smelled of fish, which made him feel somewhat nauseous, he was glad not to have to call for a taxi. He had to wait for some time for the next train but he sat in the buffet and drank two cups of strong coffee and had some hot buttered toast. Feeling better he bought a newspaper and waited in the corner of the buffet where it was warm, with only that and his briefcase bulging with his toiletry bag. He decided to ring Susan later at her flat and ask her to thank her parents for all they had done, including having dried his suit after the beach episode. He looked down at it and was thankful that Susan had brought it to the hospital when she visited him there, otherwise he would still be in the hospital unable to dress. The train arrived and Andrew slept most of the way to Liverpool Street Station.

Back at work he and Harry ate lunch together in the canteen, while he related to his friend the events of the past two days, which now seemed like weeks ago. Andrew had seen his boss who thought he looked pale and tired and insisted that Andrew go home for the rest of the day. Andrew told Harry that he had provisionally arranged for them both to go with Reggie for a trial run out to sea in the *Maggie* on Thursday afternoon, when they were both free.

'What if Susan's parents are down by the harbour and see you?' Harry suggested.

'Well, I've asked Reggie to take the boat round the other side and moor her at Walberswick, he's got a mooring over there and the river's fairly wide. We should be safe there, and it's not so far for us to travel' Andrew explained.

'And if you're seen? You'll have to have some sort of explanation up your sleeve'

Andrew thought quickly, 'Then I'll say it was a last minute invitation from a friend to go fishing' he said.

'You'd better wear a false beard till we get out of the harbour, I'll wear a mask!'

'I'll see you tomorrow then. On Thursday I'll go home for lunch and change and pick you up from Redbridge Station. It'll save me coming down to Leyton and we'll be on the A12 already to go up to Suffolk. Be there at half past one. Don't be late. It's not easy to park near the station so look out for my car. We have to be up there about three to get the tide.'

'Cheers Andy, I hope the boat is a good one, and cheap, as I'm paying for it!'

'I'll give you my share when I can. The old boy says it's sea-worthy at least,' Andrew said, hoping Harry wouldn't expect too great a bargain. He wished he had asked Reggie to clean it up a bit before Harry saw it on Thursday. The friends parted and Andrew took himself home to bed. He still felt weak and exhausted.

Back at home he rang Susan at her flat, and realised she would probably still be at her parent's home. He rang there and found she had gone to the hospital in Lowestoft to see Johnny and his mother, and had rung the Southwold hospital earlier to find he had left for work. *No doubt Susan will ring when she gets back*, he thought.

Chapter Five

Susan drove from the hospital to the promenade, parked her car and wandered down to the beach. The wind was cold on her face but she didn't mind. She drew in a deep breath and looked out to sea. Then she bent down and picked up a few flattish pebbles and threw them one by one into the water above the breakwater to try and make them skip over the surface as she had done as a child. She succeeded with two of them and smiled to herself. It reminded her of the Dam buster's film showing the 'bouncing ball' Barnes Wallis devised for blowing up the German dams during the war.

After a short, brisk walk towards the pier she turned and made her way back to the car feeling a good deal refreshed. She found renewed energy and lost the traces of depression she had felt since ringing the hospital to find Andrew gone. *It blows the cobwebs away*, Susan thought.

When Susan got home she heard that Andrew had phoned and was at home feeling exhausted. She rang him straight away.

'He says he went to work and was too tired to stay so left at lunch time and went home to bed, poor dear,' Susan told her parents, as she entered the lounge. Robert was resting on his bed but came down to tea when he heard his sister's voice downstairs.

'You look a lot better, Rob,' Susan said, staring at his face. She went on to tell them about her visit to the hospital and found Alice and Johnny Harrison.

'I wonder if she has enough to live on, perhaps we can help in some way,' Jill commented, frowning.

'I doubt if she would accept, she might think it's charity,' Bob said.

'It would be too,' Robert smiled.

'I wouldn't be proud. I'd be only too glad to accept if I knew the giver had plenty and could well afford it,' Jill reasoned.

'It's often those who can't afford it who give most,' Bob said.

'We can't generalise,' Susan remarked, 'We can keep in touch with them and help in some way or another if she wishes it.'

'Wise old thing!' Robert said, looking at his sister.

The family ate their tea which included the Christmas cake Jill had made earlier for Robert's home coming. It was meant for Sunday, but the previous day had been so eventful no one had even thought of eating Christmas cake, nor would have wanted to if they had. They had all been utterly exhausted.

'I shan't make another for Christmas day. We are usually too full with lunch to eat it,' Jill said, cutting a large slice for Robert.

'Thanks goodness for that,' teased her husband, 'or we'd be eating it every day for a month, as usual.'

'You do exaggerate, dear,' Jill smiled.

They enjoyed the quiet evening together at home. Jill and Bob had planned to take their son and daughter out for dinner for a treat but, though Susan and Robert had recovered somewhat, neither were in a fit state to go out in the cold night air. They ate cold turkey and pickles for their evening meal to save Jill having to cook, after which they watched the 9 o'clock news over coffee and liqueurs.

'How lucky are we, to be able to sit here together in peace and comfort while so many others in the world are suffering,' Jill thought aloud.

'Are you going to be posted nearer to here soon, or will you have to stay in Aldershot?' Bob asked his son, transferring his thoughts from the outside world to their own small one.

'I've no idea yet,' Robert informed him.

'Have you any idea where you might be sent to next?' his mother asked.

'No, it could be anywhere.'

That night Susan kissed her brother good night and said she would return at the weekend sometime so that she could see him again before he left the following Monday. The next morning she departed early, after taking cups of tea to her parents but not waking her brother. She went straight to her office and spent the day catching up with the backlog of work. The rest of the staff were intrigued to hear Susan's account of the sea rescue by her fiancé and of how her brother, too, had saved the boy's life.

'They ought to get a medal,' one of her staff said.

At the end of the working day Susan went straight home and rang Andrew at his flat. She was glad to find him in and they chatted about the weekends past events.

'When can we meet? I haven't seen you since your brave deed, I miss you,' she told him.

'I'll pop round tomorrow evening. I must go to work in the morning, I haven't been today. I felt so exhausted and my stomach hasn't been very comfortable. I think I swallowed rather a lot of sea water,' Andrew explained.

'Poor darling, I'll make you a nice meal tomorrow night, I'm looking forward to seeing you.'

'Same here, I'm glad you had a relaxing time with your brother. Sleep well, my love,' Andrew said, and they rang off.

Susan felt more elated than she had done the day before. After a shower and a snack she got into bed. Her mind was so full of the events of the past few days that she could not sleep. One moment her inside seemed to heave with happiness while reminiscing at the joy she felt at seeing her brother again after so long, then in turn in meeting Andrew as he had driven into the drive at her parents' home, and above all at how brave her fiancé and her brother had been down at the beach last Sunday.

Countering this her mind floated back to her disappointment at finding Andrew had left in such a hurry from the hospital, 'why so elusive?' she asked herself but found no explanation, except that he had to account only for himself for so long. She hoped this attitude would change once they were married. She felt that she had a little ladder inside her and that her emotions were climbing up it when she was elated, and running down it to the pit of her stomach when she was depressed. *I ought to be happily making plans for the wedding and going to the shops to get some idea of the sort of dress I shall wear instead of being dubious of Andrew's character*, she thought, frowning at herself. She tossed and turned and longed to have Andrew in her arms to dispel any feelings of doubt about him.

The next moment, it seemed to her, she was getting ready for work. She made a list of the food she had to buy on her way home in the evening to prepare the meal Andrew was to share with her. In the daytime Susan always found the burdens of her nights somewhat diminished, and went cheerfully off to work.

In the evening, on her arrival home from work, Susan rang her family to tell them Andrew was better and coming to dinner. He arrived just as she was putting the moussaka, she knew he enjoyed so much, into the oven. He looked no worse for his ordeal and had lost none of his ardour, he swept her up in his arms so that her feet dangled above the floor and hugged her to him. Putting her down again he looked into her face and pressed his lips onto hers, holding her head in his hands.

'My Love, it's good to see you again', he smiled, releasing her.

'It seems such a long time since we were together on the beach,' Susan said, squeezing his arm as they went into the lounge.

Andrew pulled her onto the sofa, drew her to him and their arms entwined about each other. They kissed passionately. He suddenly stood up, swept her into his arms and carried her upstairs to her bedroom. Smiling and looking deeply into one another's eyes they began to undress each other. Unable to wait Andrew bent and kissed her navel and lifted her legs onto the bed. He stroked her thighs and kissed her all over until she pulled him to her, ready to receive him and encased him tightly in her embrace. An hour later, they showered together, dressed and went down to dinner. The moussaka was well done and while Susan was dishing up Andrew poured two glasses of Pinot Noir at the dining table.

'To you, my Darling', Andrew raised his glass.

'To us,' Susan said smiling and consciously erasing her earlier doubts. She felt a great deal happier and more relaxed than she had done since she walked arm in arm along the beach with Andrew and her brother.

Andrew left very early the next morning after they had eaten breakfast together. He planned to come see Susan and her family again that following Saturday afternoon.

'Then I'll see Robert as well and leave in the evening so that you can be with him on his last weekend at home,' he reasoned with her. Susan kissed him at the front door and thanked him for his consideration.

Chapter Six

'What have you been up to today, Darling?' Susan smiled as she came in with the tea, 'It's nice to see you so early for a change'

'I thought we might go window shopping, we'll catch them still open if we hurry,' Andrew said, taking the tea she handed him.

'What's the hurry? I thought we could do that on Thursday as planned when the shops will be open till late,' Susan said, looking at him.

'I can't make Thursday now, some friends have asked me to go fishing with them.' Andrew lifted his cup to his mouth to hide his face.

'I might have known there was something in it,' Susan said in a disappointed tone of voice. They finished their tea and Susan got up without saying anything, took the tray to the kitchen, and went to get her coat. She felt let down by Andrew again. She had looked forward to going to the West End on Thursday, searching together for ideas for their new home. She cheered up somewhat while they were out, however, making the most of the time they had together. Andrew took her out to dinner to compensate, feeling relieved that Susan had made little fuss of his change of plans. Back at the flat, she unpacked the few things they had found time to buy before the shops closed. Susan laid them out on the sofa for a second inspection. She felt quite excited as she matched the colour scheme of blue and dusky pink for the bedroom.

'I can't wait to get into those fresh cotton sheets,' Andrew smiled.

'One track mind!' Susan laughed, 'Once we've found a flat we can measure up the windows for the curtains. I love that floral pattern we examined. They would look so fresh, yet warm,' she said.

'We'll buy a nice flat a bit further out, perhaps Hampstead,'

'That's a bit ambitious,' Susan said, taken aback, 'We'll never be able to afford that, to rent, let alone buy.'

'We'll see,' Andrew said quietly.

'We mustn't be too extravagant in buying anything,' Susan emphasized, 'a flat included. As long as it's big enough to have a spare room in it, I don't mind where it is, within reason,' she added.

'Spare room for guests or baby?' He remarked, smiling.

'Whichever comes first,' she returned his smile.

'Let's try for a baby as soon as we can,' Andrew suggested, 'then by the time we get married it will almost be here. We shan't have to wait so long.'

'Don't be silly Darling; I can't get married six or seven months pregnant! Whoever heard of a maternity wedding gown?' she laughed

'You could make one to fit,' Andrew said, glancing at her tummy. 'Anyway, let's go to bed, I must be at work early in the morning, I can't waste my beauty sleep and I know how demanding you are in bed, I get little sleep as it is!' he said, trying to look serious.

'Saucy tonight, aren't we!' Susan smiled as they packed up their new possessions and took them upstairs. As the lovers lay talking in each other's arms before going to sleep, Susan asked,

'Will you be able to come up to Southwold at any time over the weekend Darling? I'm going up on the Friday evening to be with Robert during his last weekend at home.'

'Of course, I'd like to but it will be a short visit. I'll drive up on Saturday afternoon and return late evening. Then you will have time to be with Robert on your own for his last day. You'd better ring your parents first and see if that will be OK. They might have other plans for you.'

'I'll ring them on Thursday evening. I am not coming home after work tomorrow. Margaret and I are going to a friends for drinks to celebrate something or other, then she and I are having dinner at her place,' Susan felt a peevish satisfaction at being able to tell Andrew this, after his plan to do his own thing on Thursday, but Andrew was asleep, or pretended to be, Susan was not sure.

Chapter Seven

*A*ndrew met Harry at Redbridge Station at 1.30pm, as planned. They drove along the A12 to Southwold. Andrew had hoped to get there to see the old craft beforehand to clear her up a bit before Harry saw her, but he'd had no time in the day and he did not fancy driving up alone after work on a dark night to do so. He still felt far from optimistic from Harry's reaction when he saw the boat. *At least Harry was glad it cost less than he had anticipated,* Andrew thought, *so perhaps he won't expect too much.*

Reggie was on the deck of the *Maggie* when they arrived at it on foot. Andrew had parked the car behind the building where he hoped it would not be seen by members of Susan's family, should they be out walking near the harbour. Andrew introduced Harry as Reggie jumped ashore to meet them.

'Come on board,' he said, swinging his arms toward the deck, inviting the two men to go first. Harry said nothing. Andrew kept his eyes diverted from his, awaiting nervously for his reaction.

'It could do with a coat of paint,' Harry said at last, as he cast his eyes over the galley, 'what's the engine like? That's the most important part,' he asked as he lifted the cover of the engine box.

'It's a good one, almost new,' Reggie lied again. He had rubbed it all down with an oil rag since Andrew had last seen it, and, indeed, it looked better for it.

'We'd better get cracking,' Reggie suggested, 'The tide is coming in and we need to get back before it ebbs, they're high at present, and it flows out fast once it starts,' he informed them. Andrew picked up the haversack of food and beer from the stern where he had laid it and placed it on the foredeck where they could reach it from the wheel. Harry started the engine on the third attempt, much to Andrew and Reggie's relief. Reggie unleashed the rope from the mooring adeptly and the boat chugged noisily on its way. Harry and Andrew wished it were a little quieter. They also felt somewhat uneasy as they passed the ferry point and could see the 'bottleneck' opening between the groynes ahead and the sea stretching between them.

Andrew stood on the mid deck watching the water as the boat cut through the small waves against the swift incoming tide, causing gurgling lapping noises along the sides and leaving a foamy path in its wake. Suddenly he heard his name being called from the car park. He recognised the voice at once as Robert's. A cold sweat came over him, and without looking to where Robert stood he dived below deck, cursing.

'What the hell's up with him? Not sea sick already I hope,' Reggie said, steering the boat towards the narrow exit. Neither man had heard Robert's call above the noise of the engine.

'Can't think.' Harry said no more, nor did he go below to find out. He concentrated on watching Reggie manoeuvre the craft through the gap and into the open sea. Andrew came back up on deck looking irritated. Harry was, by this time, at the wheel following Reggie's instructions regarding the direction he wanted to take them in. without diverting his eyes from the way ahead, he asked,,

'What's wrong with you, Andy?'

'Nothing, forget it,' Andrew did not want to explain to Harry in Reggie's presence. Harry sensed this and dropped the matter. He opened the throttle. The throb quickened and the boat skimmed over the surface more smoothly.

'She certainly moves,' Harry commented. This cheered Andrew. He began to think they had bought a good bargain and he breathed a sigh of relief on that score. Both men relaxed and took advantage of the fresh air, a big contrast to the polluted air of London. After an hour of riding the waves toward the flat-water horizon Reggie advised Harry to turn and face homewards.

'We must get back before the tide turns. It can be a bloody nuisance if the ebb is very strong, as it will be today,' he reminded them, 'You saw how narrow the entrance is. The water fairly sweeps round the groynes, since the defences were put up. There are sand banks out there, which are always changing. If you get on one of them, you're in trouble. I'll give you a chart to show you where they mainly are. You must keep to the channel coming in all costs, no matter how the tide is flowing,' he stressed.

'We must remember that', Harry said, glancing at Andrew.

'I'm telling you, you'd better,' Reggie emphasised.

Andrew handed him another can of beer, his sixth. Harry wondered if this was wise. He had decided to hand the wheel to Reggie before they entered the harbour so that he and Andrew could remember the position of the deep run of the channel.

From what Reggie had been telling them he needs to be sober, Harry reasoned to himself.

As they neared the harbour the sun was already losing height and power and Harry was glad to hand the steering back to Reggie. He pointed out where to look for sand banks. They watched the silt carrying water, fast flowing its way out of the mouth of the harbour as if longing for the freedom of the sea.

'Now you can take her as far as the mooring and I'll show you the best way to ease her home,' Reggie told Harry. He then eased down the throttle and they slid towards the mooring in subdued light. Andrew had already made himself scarce by starting to clear up the empty cans and going below deck, an excuse to hide, in case Robert or any of the family was about.

Reggie steered the *Maggie* beyond its mooring and easily turned her to face the harbour mouth, as she was when they had boarded her. They gently touched the old car tyres Reggie had hung over the side of the landing stage to provide a soft landing for the craft. Andrew came up and smiled to himself, thinking they could hardly damage the paintwork. Reggie shut off the engine, threw the 'painter' loop over the bollard, and nimbly jumped ashore. He pulled the vessel tightly against the side and fastened the stern onto the second bollard. Andrew jumped ashore carrying the empties and the sandwich box. Harry followed. Both men felt unsteady on their feet after two hours of sea motion.

'Always turn her ready for the next trip, then you can get off quicker and you don't have to worry so much about the other boats. This river gets a bit crowded at times, especially in the summer, Reggie warned them.

'Well, what do you think?' He asked, 'A good old craft, isn't she?' he added before they had time to express their opinion. He looked from one to the other to get their reactions, while at the same time stuffing his hands deep down into his trouser pockets to give himself more confidence and a nonchalant air.

'Well, she seems OK. She's sound, so with a coat of paint she should serve us for fishing trips,' Harry said, looking at Andrew for his opinion. Andrew felt relieved on Harry's verdict. They bartered a while with Reggie on the price and an amicable settlement was reached after he had tried and failed to be paid in cash. He still offered to keep his eye on the boat, hoping to gain a bit more from them from time to time in doing so.

Andrew and Harry drove too fast down the A12 towards London, stopping at a pub for a hot snack en route. They discussed the difficulties in keeping the boat in the harbour at Walberswick without being recognised again by members of Susan's family. The state of the *Maggie* necessitated visiting her at frequent intervals. Her paintwork needed renewing and the cabin made more comfortable. They decided too that some of the ropes would have to be replaced and the engine serviced to ensure their safety at sea. By the time they reached town they both felt very tired and decided to go their separate ways.

'Are you seeing Susan tonight?' Harry asked.

'No, I'll give her a ring from the flat and turn in early,' Andrew said.

'Where will you say you have been if she asks?'

'I've already told her I was fishing with friends,' Andrew informed him, smiling.

'And if she fishes for more detail you'll have to fish in your fish brain for a story that doesn't sound too fishy!' teased Harry with a cocky smile.

'Bugger off! Call yourself a friend?' Andrew laughed, giving him a shove as Harry opened the car door to get out. He slammed it shut and waved to Andrew as the car sped off in the direction of Chigwell.

Chapter Eight

*I*n the meantime, Robert's cold had come to nothing. He had rested in his parents company and realising his holiday was slipping by decided to walk over to Walberswick to see his old school chum, John Hammond. They had always kept in touch since he had left Sizewell, nearby, in protest of extending the plant.

John was at home when Robert rang him and was pleased to get out and walk to meet Robert across the bridge. The cold wind had died down and a soft breeze from the south blew gently across Robert's face as he made his way along the promenade and down to the harbour. He saw John from a distance and waved to him as he came towards him, from the direction of the footbridge. They smiled and hastened towards one another, shaking hands firmly when they met.

'Good to see you mate', John said, patting Robert on the shoulder with his free hand.

'It's good to see you too,' Robert said, as they looked each other up and down.

'What are you up to? How long do you have this time? When did you arrive?' John asked, all in one breath.

'I came home last week, I've got another week,' Robert informed him.

'Jolly good, I'm still without work. I have an interview with an electronics firm in Norwich next week. It's difficult to get a job if you have rocked the boat at all, so to speak,' John told him.

'Do you really think the nuclear plant is that dangerous?' Robert asked, feeling doubtful about it.

'God, yes,' John frowned, looking at him, 'If there was a nuclear war it wouldn't make much difference. We'd all be goners anyway and if we had a conventional war again a bomb on that would have the same effect,' he said. 'It would be worse than the Chernobyl disaster,' and added, 'If an enemy got in the plant he could do untold damage, besides the fact that anything could go wrong at any time. Humans aren't infallible, and nor are the machines for that matter'.

Robert began to feel a bit depressed. He tried to cheer John up by joking,

'Don't worry John, I'll come and save the old country!' he said smiling.

'Huh! You'll probably be saving some other poor buggers in another country, till it reached them,' John said, gazing across the harbour. Robert followed his gaze. An old fishing boat was slowly chugging past them. The two friends had wandered, while talking, as afar as they could venture on the north side of the river. They stood still to watch the craft cutting slowly through the turbulent water out towards the sea. Suddenly, Robert drew in a deep breath. He could not at first believe his eyes. He strained to get a better view. Running to the edge of the water, he yelled,

'Andrew!'

'Who's that?' John asked, as Robert stared after the boat

'What the hell!' Robert gasped, 'What the hell?' he repeated in disbelief. On hearing his name across the water, Andrew swore, put his head down, and disappeared below deck.

'What the hell is he doing over here in that boat?' Robert asked himself.

'Don't give it names old Boy, an old tub, it's hardly seaworthy,' John commented.

'That was my sister's fiancé. I'd like to know what the blazes he's doing out there,' Robert almost shouted, his eyes still following the now tiny speck of the boat as it crossed the bar of the river and disappeared out to sea.

'What the hell is going on, I'd like to know. He must have seen me, why didn't he acknowledge me for god's sake?' Robert said, shaking his head and turning away from the mouth of the estuary as if he had forgotten John and was talking to himself.

'He's probably going fishing with friends, what are you so surprised about?' John asked.

'I was with him last Sunday; he's never been around this area before he met Susan. She told me she'd shown him round when he came to stay with my parents last month,' Robert explained.

'What do you think he's up to then?' John asked, without thought.

'How would I know,' Robert frowned. 'It's Thursday, why isn't he working? I wonder if Susan knows. It's a mystery to me' he went on.

'Is it a case of mistaken identity? Perhaps it wasn't him. You could be wrong. I wouldn't worry about it if I were you' John said.

'I know it was him. Come on, let's have a cup of tea somewhere,' Robert said, walking towards the town. They walked in silence up Ferry Road and took the short cut over the sandy hump to Gun Hill path and dropped down to the promenade.

'I saved a little kids life along here last week,' Robert told John after wondering whether to tell him or not. He thought it would take his mind off Andrew and give them something else to talk about. John looked at him quizzically, 'You really did?' He said, for the second time making an inane remark.

'Yes, but only after Andrew had swum in after him,' Robert added, not wanting to sound boastful.

'Good God! Not that bloke you saw on the boat?' John explained inanely again. Robert was beginning to think his friend had lost his power of conversation, and a feeling of irritation began to swell up inside of him.

'Of course, I told you he was here last week,' he reminded John.

'How did you do it?' John asked, with emphasis. Robert smiled, but felt like kicking some sense into his friend.

'I turned him upside down and shook the water out of him, then gave him artificial resuscitation with my bicycle pump,' Robert said, sarcastically, not knowing whether to laugh or scream at his friend. John took no offence and just laughed.

'Ask a stupid question, eh?! He said

The two friends had tea in town and Robert walked as far as South Green with his friend.

'Cheerio old Boy, jolly nice to see you again,' John said, shaking Robert's hand.

'Good to see you too John. I hope you have some luck finding a job. Let me know how you get on,' Robert said.

'I will, and by the way, next time you give a kid artificial resuscitation, use a foot pump, it'll be quicker!' he smiled as they turned to go.

'Touché,' Robert laughed, and waved to John over his shoulder.

As Robert walked hurriedly back towards home alone his mind returned to Andrew and the boat. He wondered whether to tell his parents, or whether he should telephone Susan and hear what she has to say about the matter. He had not made up his mind by the time he reached home, so kept quiet for the time being.

'Hello Son, how was John?' Jill asked as he walked into the kitchen where she was preparing the evening meal.

'OK, he hasn't got a job yet,' Robert told her. He took off his outdoor shoes and waded into the lounge in his stockinged feet.

'Back then? How did you find John?' His father asked.

'He's going for an interview for another job next week,' Robert told him.

'Oh! Doesn't he like being at Sizewell anymore?' Bob asked.

'No, he left there a while ago,' Robert said, not wanting to explain further exactly why John left. He couldn't be bothered to get into an argument on the pros and cons of nuclear fuel. He had Andrew on his mind still.

'Have a drink Son,' Bob offered.

'Thanks, I will. What can I pour for you, Dad?' He enquired.

'My usual, an Adnams,' he smiled at Robert.

'What will you have to drink, Mum? Robert called to his mother from the hall.

'A dry sherry, Love, please,' she called back, 'leave it in there, I'll be in in a minute.'

Robert poured the drinks and sat at his usual seat, facing the fireplace. He watched the flames eating away at the large logs in the grate, wishing his mind felt as relaxed as the surrounding atmosphere. His mother walked in, bringing a waft of cooked chicken with her. She picked up her sherry and sat down opposite her husband.

Funny how one gets used to same chair and the same position, Robert thought, *when I get married I'll call 'all change,' and get everyone moving round one* he mused.

'Where did you meet John?' Jill asked, for something to say.

'By the harbour as he came over the foot bridge,' Robert told her. Silence fell once more.

'You are quiet, you seem subdued,' Jill said, looking at Robert and sensing an atmosphere. Robert took the cue almost before he realised it and heard himself explaining to Jill and Bob what he had seen.

'Are you sure it was Andrew?' Bob said, sitting up and putting down his 'Times' crossword.

'Yes I am,' Robert stressed.

'I can't think what he could be doing out there, unless he's gone fishing with a friend,' Bob suggested,

'Then why didn't he acknowledge me?' Robert wondered.

'Perhaps he didn't see you,' Jill said.

'I'm sure he did, he must have heard me call him,' Robert reasoned.

'We'd better phone Susan and ask her. She might have a simple explanation,' Bob said, getting out of his seat.

'Wait a minute!' Jill suddenly exclaimed 'she did tell me, when they were here, that he had thought of buying a yacht. That was after they had been for a walk over the bridge to Walberswick. Perhaps he's trying one out in secret,' she explained.

'The thing they were on wasn't a yacht by any stretch of the imagination. John called it a tub. He went as far to say it wasn't seaworthy,' Robert said.

'He wouldn't have gone out in it if it hadn't been, I shouldn't have thought. He seems to have his head screwed on,' Bob commented with his usual cliché. He sat down in his chair again until a decision was reached.

'I don't suppose he wants to spend much money on a new boat as they are planning to get married next year.' Jill reasoned.

'Perhaps he's buying it for Susan as a surprise for Christmas,' Bob suggested. They all laughed.

'Well, perhaps it's best not to interfere. We might be letting the cat out of the bag if we ring her,' Jill said, restraining her impulses to get on the phone straight away to ring her daughter.

They ate their chicken dinner with little conversation, each of them with their minds enveloped in the mystery of Andrew's boat trip. At one point Bob began to think it possible that Robert made a mistake in identity, but kept his thoughts to himself, Jill worried that he might waste money on buying a boat at this time when they would need all their savings in setting up their home together after marriage. Robert had a niggling feeling there was something underhand in what Andrew was doing, he visualised recurrently the moment he had called to Andrew, who not only ignored him, but disappeared like a rabbit down a hole.

Jill brought in the dessert just as the phone rang.

'I'll go, I'm up,' she said, and hurried into the hall. It was Susan.

'Hello Mum,' she sounded happy. 'Is it all right if Andrew comes up for the afternoon on Saturday? He wants to see Robert again before he goes away.'

'Of course, Darling, is he with you now?' Jill asked, hoping Andrew was back from his boat trip and she might hear some explanation from Susan that would put their mind at rest, but none was forthcoming.

'No, he asked me when he was here last Tuesday evening,' she told her mother, careful not to say 'night'. 'He kindly thought we might like Robert's last night en famille,' she added.

'That's kind. Is everything all right?' Jill asked, fishing for any information that would give those clues.

'Yes, everything is fine, Andrew has fully recovered,' Susan said, thinking that was why her mother sounded worried.

'Good,' Jill said, wearily, 'We look forward to seeing you both. Are you coming up Friday night by yourself or coming with Andrew on Saturday?' She asked.

'I'll be up on Friday evening in time for dinner. I shall need the car anyway, to get back on Sunday night.' Susan was beginning to wonder what else was on her mother's mind. *I just told her we would be together on Robert's last weekend*, she thought, irritation welling up within her.

'Oh yes! Of course, silly me. We look forward to seeing you, Darling. We're in the middle of dinner so I'll ring off. Goodnight.' She put down the receiver and went back to the dining room where Bob and Robert had finished eating and were resting back in their chairs.

'No hints concerning Andrew?' Bob asked.

'No, he's coming up on Saturday to see Robert,' She

informed him. Robert raised his eyebrows and looked across at his father.

'That will be a bit awkward. I wonder if he will mention the boat trip,' Robert said.

'We'd better not mention it in case Andrew wants it to be a surprise for Susan', Jill said, hopefully.

'Right, and we'll have to try and put it out of our minds when Susan arrives tomorrow,' Bob advised.

'God, I wish I'd never noticed him,' Robert said, frowning, and got up to clear the table.

Chapter Nine

On his way to see Susan and her family two days later Andrew worked round and round in his mind what to tell them if Robert had informed them he had seen him on the boat. If the matter did not arise, he would not mention it but if it did, he would say he was fishing with friends as he said he would be. He did not want to tell them he was buying the boat with a friend. They might think it a strange thing to do just before getting married and odd too that he was so near to Susan's family without telling Susan from where he was fishing. He realised the folly in suggesting Southwold harbour to Harry, it would have been better if they had found another, further away. He had thought it would be convenient in the future to get away with Harry sometimes while Susan was with her parents.

The thought also entered his mind that he could tell Robert it was a case of mistaken identity. After all, he figured, Thursday afternoon was a normal working time for most people. He would have to 'play it by ear'. All the same, he drove with a feeling of trepidation as he neared Southwold.

Susan ran out to meet him at his car as he pulled into the drive of her parents' home.

'Hi, Darling, it good to see you,' Susan put her arms tightly around Andrew's neck as he tried to climb out of the car.

'Help!, Rape!' he cried, 'give me a chance to straighten up!' he laughed. 'There, now let me look at you. You look great, as usual,' he said, holding her at arm's length, then pulling her towards him and kissed her on the lips.

'Steady on. Come on inside, out of the cold, you two. Hello Andrew, good to see you,' Bob said, shaking his hand.

'Nice to see you too, Bob,' the two lovers followed him indoors; their arms entwined, and glanced at each other, smiling.

They all exchanged greetings and Andrew handed Jill a large box of chocolates from his overcoat pocket before taking it off.

'Where's mine?' Susan asked, holding out her hand, with her chin in the air.

'They're not good for fiancées,' he smiled.

'On the contrary,' Jill corrected him, 'that's often the only time girls get them!' they went into the lounge where Bob was by then standing warming his backside in front of the fire.

'Robert will be back in a moment. He's gone to the shop for me, I forgot the milk, and I do hate shopping on a Sunday, don't you?' Andrew often had to go to the shop on Sundays when he ran out of something so did not reply to her comment.

Jill retired to the kitchen to prepare tea as Robert came in slamming the front door and joined her. He called, 'Hi Andrew,' having seen his car in the drive. To Andrew's relief nothing was mentioned by Robert, of seeing him on the boat until they were alone for a while in the late evening. Dinner was over and Bob had deliberately gone to help Jill and Susan to wash up the coffee cups and liqueur glasses while the dishwasher pumped away the remains of the dinner from the plates. Robert sensed Bob's motive and using the opportunity, said,

'Andrew, may I ask you something?' Andrew tried to smile and look casual, having an idea what Robert was going to say. Without waiting for a reply, Robert asked him,

'Why did you not acknowledge me when I called to you on that fishing boat the other day?'

'For two reasons,' Andrew started to explain in a whisper, his hands tightly entwined behind his back, 'Firstly, it was a secret mission,' and Andrew went on to tell Robert in brief what it was but asked him not to mention it to his parents or to Susan. He explained that he wished to familiarise himself with the harbour as he wanted at some point to buy a small dinghy or even a yacht as a surprise for Susan. He ended by asking, somewhat nervously,

'Did you tell your parents you had seen me?'

'I told them, yes, but not Susan, as we guessed you didn't want her to know and you would tell her yourself in good time. We guessed rightly about the boat at least,' Robert said quietly and smiled.

'Thank goodness for that,' Andrew said, with a greater sense of relied than Robert could realise.

'Who was with you?' Andrew suddenly asked, remembering that Robert had not been alone on Osprey Quay.

'Oh! That was John, a friend of mine. He thought it was a case of wrong identification. He will have forgotten it by now,' Robert assured Andrew.

'Then tell your parents to do the same, please. I don't want it leaked to Susan,' Andrew told him.

'Will you have another drink?' Robert asked in a louder tone of voice than they had been using.

'No thanks, I must hit the road. I've probably had more than the limit for driving as it is,' as Susan entered the lounge, surprised he was going so soon.

'It's not yet half past nine,' she said, looking up into his face.

'I know, but I have to be at work early tomorrow', he told her, taking her face in his hands and kissing the tip of her nose. He turned to Robert with an outstretched hand.

'Good luck Robert, I hope all goes well. We'll see you back soon?' they shook hands.

'Cheers Andrew. I hope to get back for the wedding.'

'You must!' Bob and Jill said in unison.

'Yes, I can't get married without my dear brother present,' Susan said, putting an arm through his. Jill and Bob shook hands with Andrew and Susan accompanied him to the car.

'Did you manage to get any idea of what he was up to on that boat?' Bob asked quietly, while Jill stood near, all ears.

'It's all right, just as we thought, so keep it quiet. He was fishing and wants to know the harbour for when he buys a dinghy for Susan to sail.'

'She used to sail from the beach on a calm day, you remember. It was easier and quicker than tacking out of the harbour first,' Jill said. They heard the car rev up and fade away and so sat down looking composed when Susan came in.

'I'm glad he came up again before you go back,' she told Robert. She sank back in her chair with her arms dangling over the back of her head.

'Yes, it was good of him to make the effort,' Robert said.

'Don't worry, it's only because I'm here!' she teased.

'No doubt about that, of course!' he retorted.

'At what time do you have to leave on Monday morning?' Jill asked him.

'About seven I think. I have to catch the train to Liverpool Street and get to Paddington to meet some mates and catch the next train from there about eleven o'clock.'

'You could come down with me. I wouldn't mind leaving earlier on Monday morning. I could go back then instead of tomorrow evening,' Susan suggested.

'No, don't do that. You would have to drop me at the underground station anyway. Thanks all the same.'

'It's OK, Lad, we can take you all the way to Liverpool Street at least. Then we'll have a little more time with you,' Bob said, looking over his newspaper.

'No thanks, Dad; it'll be a worry in all that rush hour traffic. I must be at Paddington on time. The trains and the underground are more reliable,' Robert told his father. Nor did he want his mother kissing him on the cheek and calling him 'Darling' in front of his mates.

'Thanks for that remark, Rob,' Bob said, pretending to pout, while his mother, disappointed, frowned slightly.

'Oh, you know what I mean, Pa. If you drop me off at our station I will be grateful.

'That goes without saying,' Bob said, going back to reading his paper.

They sat for a while enjoying each other's company and the comfort of the log fire. *A rare occasion*, Susan thought. At 10.30, Robert got up and excused himself, saying, 'Goodnight,' and kissing his mother on the cheek.

'I think I'll go too', Susan told them as she jumped up, 'I'm tired, I'll leave you two in peace,'

'We sit here in peace too often,' Jill told her as Susan bent to kiss her. Susan felt a twinge of sadness for them, especially as Robert was about to leave them again for another long period. As she climbed the stairs, she decided to stay the Sunday night so they could all be together for another long evening and she could be there to see Robert before he left.

The family enjoyed Robert's last day with them and rose early on the Monday morning to have breakfast with him. As it was, his mother spent most of the time in her kitchen packing sandwiches for him. Susan crept downstairs looking bleary eye.

'You ought to be in the Army. You'd get used to having to wake up as soon as you get out of bed, no time to wander about like a little zombie!' He teased.

'I'd never do it. I'd be on jankers every day,' Susan said, trying hard to focus on her food.

'Hello, Darling, did you sleep well?' Jill asked, entering the room with the toast rack over-flowing.

'Shush! She's still asleep, don't wake her,' Robert whispered, reaching for the toast at the same time as Bob.

'I had to get up to see Rob off,' Susan mumbled, rubbing her face.

'You'll have to open those peepers a bit wider to do that,' he told her. He got up from the table, and addressing his father, excused himself and ran upstairs two at a time to complete his packing.

Jill sat down, looking miserable. Susan looked at her and said, 'Cheer up, Ma, He'll be back again soon.' She reached across the table and patted her mother's hand to comfort her.

'I wish he was stationed nearer and not at the other side of London,' she said.

'You know, it takes longer to get to many other places. The train is fast. It's lucky I'm not in the north of Scotland or abroad somewhere,' Robert told her.

'You could be in Paris quicker than in Aldershot, all the same,' his father said, looking over the top of his newspaper.

'I'd die of fright at the entrance of the Channel Tunnel,' Jill told him.

'It'll probably feel like being in the underground. You don't mind that,' Bob said, putting down the morning paper at last and joining the conversation.

'I couldn't bear to think of all that deep water and ships flowing over my head,' Jill reasoned.

'No! Buildings, roads and cars instead!' Susan laughed.

'Fish and ships,' Bob said, smiling.

'My, you're bright this morning. The only one who is!' Jill said.

Robert trundled downstairs with his heavy luggage bag. Bob got up and went into the garage to get the car out. Jill gave Robert his sandwiches for the journey, which he squashed as best as he could into the side pocket of his bag. His mother looked on despairingly. Susan got up from the table and put her arms around her brother's neck. They kissed each other on the cheek and said their goodbyes while Bob put the luggage in the boot of the car. Robert looked at his sister.

'Bye Sis', and good luck, I'm glad I've met Andrew, I fully approve!'

'I'm glad you like him. That means a lot to me,' she smiled.

He turned to his mother and took both her hands in his.

'Thanks, Ma, for everything. I'll see you soon; I'll ring you when I get there'.

'Goodbye, my Darling. Take good care of yourself,' Jill told him, holding back her tears. They held each other tightly for a few minutes and then, releasing her, Robert turned and joined his father in the car.

'Aren't you going with them?' Susan asked, surprised.

'No, I'll stay and see you off to work, no use prolonging the agony,' Jill said, busying herself clearing the table.

'I hope he gets home for your wedding,' she added, making her way to the kitchen with the full tray.

'I'm sure they will allow that,' Susan said, hopefully.

Chapter Ten

*A*ndrew and Harry spent many hours of their free time in Walberswick rubbing down and scraping the paint off the boat while Reggie sometimes went over in his small rowing boat to greet them and stood and watched. He considered that now the *Maggie* was sold to them he wanted no part in her restoration, except for a fee, perhaps, if the new owner's offered, which they deliberately did not. They had found the new mooring on the Walberswick side of the Blyth which Reggie had negotiated for with someone he knew. Andrew usually travelled in Harry's car to obviate recognition. He wore an old ski cap and overalls as disguise, as well as for practical purposes.

'I don't want my fiancée to know of my venture, nor her parents for that matter,' Andrew told Harry. He considered that they knew too much already. He was careful not to mention her name in front of Reggie, or give him any indication of where she lived, he did not trust him. The two men painted *Maggie* a dull blue with a sea green deck and a line of the same colour under it along the top most clinker plank. They decided to keep her name and painted it white. This pleased Reggie, but he thought it should be done in black.

'It shows up better in black,' he told them.

Jill and Bob had, indeed, wandered down to the harbour one afternoon as dusk was falling. Their walks were usually taken during the mornings when weather permitted and the cold December wind was not blowing from the east. On that morning, they had shopped for the last gifts they needed to buy for Christmas. They had lunched at The Swan and stayed to rest in the lounge before their walk.

As they wandered along westwards, hands in their pockets, thy both felt inquisitive about the sailing boat Andrew was buying for Susan.

'I don't suppose he has bought one yet, he hasn't been to see us for a few weeks,' Jill said.

'If he had, he might not come to see us, he might be afraid we'll spill the beans.'

'I don't like intrigue, it makes me feel uncomfortable inside,' Jill said, frowning.

'I doubt he will buy one till they have been married for a time anyway,' Bob said, 'so we may as well forget it.'

They went on in silence, with their private thoughts, then turned and stopped by the water to watch the gentle flow out to sea. Jill looked around at the boats and scanned the opposite bank. The late sun shone red against all that faced it to the west, and Jill put her hand up to shield her eyes and peered through them in the half darkness. Suddenly her gaze rested on a fishing boat. She grabbed Bob's arm, he looked at her, and then followed her gaze to the opposite bank.

'What's up, Darling?'

'Look!' she said, pointing to the boat with a silhouette of two men on the deck, 'I'm sure that's Andrew on that fishing boat'

'Where? I can't see him,'

'That one with the funny woolly hat, it looks just like him,' she said in a whisper, as if Andrew might hear her from the other side of the river.

'It certainly looks like his build,' Bob agreed.

'I'm sure it's him,' Jill said, as she began to wave and was about to call out to him when Bob pushed her arm down and said, urgently,

'Don't. We mustn't get involved. He might not want to see us, and anyway, it might not be him then we will look silly.' He took Jill's arm and turned her to face the town. He gently forced her in that direction against her reluctance to leave the riverside.

'That couple across there on the other side were eyeing us for some time. I think they recognised you, even in this light. Don't look now,' Harry told Andrew in a low voice.

'Oh! Bugger! Andrew glanced sideways without moving his head, 'That's them all right,' Andrew swore again, 'perhaps they haven't recognised me,' he said hopefully, as Bob and Jill turned away without acknowledging them. He moved to the starboard side of the boat quickly where he could not be seen, in case they turned round again. Bob and Jill made their way home, feeling somewhat uneasy. They eventually put their minds at rest by assuming it had not been Andrew they had seen.

'He would hardly be cleaning up an old fishing boat, especially at this time of day,' Bob concluded, convinced they had made an error in identification.

'They've gone, thank God!' Harry said. Andrew had automatically bent down and hidden his face, ostrich fashion.

'We must work on her at night,' Harry said, 'after the sun has gone down, it shone directly onto the boat across the flats.'

'It would be even colder than it is now,' Andrew said, putting down his brush and standing to stretch himself.

'We'd have to use spotlights to work by, that could cause suspicion all round.'

'We can honestly say we're hard working Londoners, unable to get away during the day, if anyone asks,' Harry said, rubbing his cold hands. 'Anyway,' he continued, 'we'll soon be finished. There's not much to do outside, and then we can work in the warmth of the cabin.

'We want to get her in the water before Christmas, there aren't many days left,' Andrew reminded his friend.

They packed up their paint, cleaned the brushes and stowed away their overalls in the cabin. Andrew lit the Calor gas burner and they ate the pork pies they had bought with them and warmed themselves with hot tea.

'It's nearly six; I must get back to the flat. I promised to ring Susan. I told her I might get over to see her tonight. It'll be too late by the time we get back to London,' Andrew remembered. 'She won't be very pleased,' he said, turning off the gas. The two men made their way to the car, just stopping to glance back once to glimpse their handiwork but could only see the silhouette of the *Maggie*. They sped back to London. Andrew rang Susan as soon as he got into the flat.

'Hello', she said, 'I've tried to ring you a number of times, where have you been? '

'Working,' Andrew, told her, in all honesty.

'Always working. When will you stop and spend an evening with me?' she said, possessively. 'I hoped you would be here for a meal tonight. You said you would try. It's late now. I've had my meal,' she went on, disappointed and upset. She refrained from telling him she had cooked for him as well.

'I'm sorry, Darling. I will pop round tomorrow evening. I finish work early. I look forward to seeing you,' he hoped for a more loving tone and forgiving words from her.

'I nearly drove over to your flat after work, so we could be together as soon as you got back from work, but I didn't want to wait in the car for ages in this climate,' Andrew was very relieved that she hadn't.

'No good doing that, ever,' he emphasized, to put her off doing so on future occasions. 'I never know what time I shall get home, precisely,'

'See you tomorrow night then. Dinner at seven o'clock, that'll make the evening longer.' Susan said no more and put the receiver down before Andrew was able to.

Andrew spent the evening disturbed by Susan's reaction as she did by his inconsistent behaviour. She hoped he would not be as unpredictable in his home coming times when they were married. She felt miserable wondering about the possibility of having to wait about in the evenings for him to walk in for meals, especially when she was still working and had to cook when she got home tired. She had always been used to punctual meal times at home. She retired to bed early and read, to take her mind off her disappointment and worries about the changes that would have to be made in her married life. She read until the early hours, until she felt tired enough to fall asleep and not lie there continuing to worry.

Chapter Eleven

A week later Andrew and Harry had the boat ready, looking as spick and span as they could get her, without the finishing touches a woman would make to the galley area. The two men purchased life jackets from the nearby chandlers, some plastic mugs and plates, a large thermos in order to have some hot water for drinks at any time, and tin kettle. They had with them some car rugs in case at some time they might be too late to get back into the harbour and would have to anchor and wait for the next tide. The two bunks up front of the cabin had them on foam mattresses that had seen better days. Harry covered these with plastic sheeting and old army blankets he had unearthed from his mother's attic. Andrew bought two cheap cushions to use as pillows if the need arose. They were arranging these when Reggie arrived from the Southwold side of the river.

'Watcha,' he greeted them, 'where are your nets, or are you only using lines?' He asked them without waiting for the return greeting the men were reluctant to give.

'Oh, we're bringing lines along tomorrow when we go out fishing,' Andrew told him. Harry wished his friend had not mentioned when they intended to go to sea. He might want to go along too which they did not want.

'I wondered 'cause I've got a couple of nets I could sell you,' Reggie said, hopefully.

'Thanks all the same,' Andrew said, not looking at Reggie and hoping he would go away.

'The tide will be OK for a good night's fishing,' Reggie told them, looking towards the harbour mouth, and hoping they would invite him along.

'But get back before seven in the morning and keep your eyes on the harbour lights. You've got your compass and the chart I gave you, have you?' he asked.

'Yes thanks, and a Decca navigator too,' Harry told him proudly.

'You won't need that if you steer due east and return due west. That is, allowing for the sand ridges I've shown you, but they'll be no problem if you come and go while the tide is in full swell. I never use a Decca,' he informed them, cockily.

'Good! Then perhaps we shan't need it,' Andrew said, beginning to feel irritable with Reggie, but at the same time half wishing they were taking him with them. He had little experience of night navigation and did not relish the thought of even looking down into the dark depths of the sea. He knew Reggie had a lifetime's experience with these waters of the East Coast, but never the less treated them with respect.

'If you get stuck on the sand banks, you'll have to wait there until the next tide,' Reggie reminded them. Andrew felt even more uneasy at that remark.

'Don't forget to take plenty of warm clothes and food,' Reggie advised, importantly. The men thanked him. Realising he had failed to persuade them to take him with them, he waved goodnight and reluctantly rowed himself back across the river in his dinghy.

'Don't forget the fuel!' he called back. The men waved from the deck in the semi darkness, peering at the silhouette of the little boat and listening to the lap lap of the oars as they entered and left the water, shining red from the reflection of lights on land.

'I hope the weather will hold for tomorrow night,' Harry said, looking up at the starlit sky.

'The forecast is good and not much wind, which will help,' Andrew said, hopefully. He went below deck to inspect the cans of diesel fuel they'd stowed away in the corner of the galley. He satisfied himself that there was enough for the trip.

Harry dropped Andrew off at his Chigwell flat and returned home to his mother who had a meal waiting for him. Andrew rang Susan and told her he would be over at the weekend and would take her out for a meal Saturday. He suggested that they went to Romany's in Jeremy Street, which is small enough to create an intimate atmosphere. He also said he'd like to stay the night at her flat, and told her, with some trepidation, that he was going night fishing with his friend Harry the night before. To his relief she seemed satisfied with that.

'I hope you will be satisfied with your catch at night when we are married, without having to go to sea!' she teased him.

'Sue, really!' Andrew laughed down the phone, but inwardly hoped that he would be able to guard some freedom, bachelor like, that he was used to now. He realised that if they had children he would have to pull his weight, so to speak, when at home and in the evenings and at weekends, especially if Susan wanted to go back to work. *Can't have it both ways,* he told himself. However, he felt a little pang of being somewhat trapped in marital commitments already, by her comment, inviting as the implication was.

'Are you still there Andrew?' Susan called down the phone, after the silence continued, caused by his inner thoughts.

'Oh! Yes, I'm looking forward to being wrapped up in your loving arms Darling,' he told her, getting back to thoughts of the immediate future.

'I'll see you Saturday then. Bye, my Love.' Susan ended the conversation and put down the phone. She, in turn, was wondering how often she would be left on her own with the children while he was out enjoying his friends and his freedom. *We'll have to arrange to have an evening out each week together,* Susan told herself. *And occasionally alone to see our friends, while the other babysits, then neither of us will feel confined,* she thought. Even then negative thoughts sauntered through her mind as she wondered if she would sit and home thinking Andrew might be with another woman. She smiled to herself as she thought to herself they'd have to continue to satisfy each other sexually as they do now. She sat down to watch television in order to sweep away anxieties. She found nothing of interest on any of the channels, so Susan took herself off to bed with the novel she was enjoying.

Chapter Twelve

After work the following evening Andrew drove up to Harry's for 6pm. He enjoyed a hot meal offered by Harry's mother Betty. Both men tried to suppress their anticipation and excitement of the boat trip before them, pretending to be matter of fact in front of her. They got their fishing tackle together and said goodbye to her in the hall.

'You two are crazy going out at this time of night, in December especially. Take good care of yourselves. I'll have a nice hot breakfast for you for when you get back. What time do you think that'll be?' she asked.

'I should think about 7.30, Ma, by the time we get back into harbour and tidy up the boat and everything,' Harry told her.

'We will ring when we're leaving Southwold, shall we, or is that too early?' Andrew suggested.

'Yes, do, any time, I'm always awake before seven, and I probably won't sleep much thinking of the two of you out there on those dark waters,' she forced a smile.

'Don't worry, Mother, have a good night's sleep so your fit enough to cook all those fish we are bringing home,' Harry said, waving to her over his shoulder as he followed Andrew to the car in the drive.

The two men drove into the darkness hoping the moon would be up by the time they reached Walberswick.

'I'm not keen on the dark deep water, I find it rather eerie,' Andrew said, wondering if the whole excursion was a good idea after all.

'It was your idea in the first place. Anyway, think of the catch and be positive,' Harry told him.

By the time they reached Blythburgh the moon was coming up and they could see the boat in front of them as they arrived at the estuary. They unloaded the car and stowed the equipment away in the hold. Harry lit the two new lanterns they had brought with them in the galley while Andrew drove the car onto some rough ground nearby. He pocketed the keys and climbed aboard the *Maggie* to join his friend. The prepared the galley ready for a snack later and opened a can of brown ale each.

'Cheers! To give us Dutch courage!' Harry smiled, lifting his can to his mouth. 'It's nearly nine o'clock, the tide is high tonight with the pull of the moon,' he continued, glancing up to where it was hanging, almost at its full, in the navy coloured sky. 'The water's on the turn now. We can go out on the ebb tide and come in, in the morning, on the flow.'

'We'd better get cracking then,' Andrew suggested, feeling still half inclined to call the whole thing off.

Harry started the engine while Andrew untied the painter and pushed the boat away from the side with one leg, nearly falling off in the process. They chugged away towards the mouth of the Blyth River, the little light on the bow seeming to guide them. They kept well into the middle as they neared the narrow exit to the sea. Harry kept the throttle in as far as possible so that the boat drifted out on the tide, saving fuel and causing the engine to make a quiet, gentle noise, almost soothing to their somewhat nervous insides. They were relieved to enter the open sea and kept a straight course towards the fishing area they had charted, about three miles offshore. Andrew peered at his watch.

'Nearly ten to ten, not bad. We soon got out of the harbour,' he said, surprised it was no later.

'We'll be there in good time,' Harry said, smiling, 'We should be able to catch a few fish before midnight, if we're lucky.'

The sea was a bit choppy with the influence of the tide still with them and a westerly breeze. This caused the boat to rock up and down as well as sideways. Andrew wondered if he would become seasick before they got to the fishing grounds, but he held on to his full stomach. Harry was more used to the rhythm of the waves and the thought did not occur to him. He enjoyed the sound of the lapping water beneath him, *like riding a horse,* he thought to himself, *hearing the rhythm of its hooves beneath you and having control of your transport.* He smiled, feeling excitement and peace alternately.

'We might get accustomed to this idea and make regular visits to the fishing grounds,' he said to Andrew.

'It would be an idea. The fishermen go out in all the weathers, but I don't think we should take chances. They are used to it, they're experts,' Andrew said, not keen to try their luck.

'Right, they've fished all their lives and some good yarns they could spin, no doubt. They could educate us townies.' Harry smiled. They studied the compass to make sure they were still on course, and found the southerly wind and current movements had caused the boat to drift slightly to the north.

'Lucky the sky is still clear, we might need the North Star yet, to set this,' Andrew said, naively, as he peered down at the compass.

'I set it before we left land, so it'll remain correct if we don't move it. For God's sake, don't do that,' Harry warned him.

He steered the *Maggie* E.S.E. for a short time then set her on course again due east. They rode the waves at a steady rate of knots till they reached the point on the chart they had aimed for, then circled the area a while but saw no other fishing vessel in sight.

'We've got this spot to ourselves, looks like,' Andrew said.

'Thank God! We should be OK here. We'll let the throttle in and get the fishing tackle,' Harry replied.

The *Maggie* slid to a gentle speed, almost stopping. Harry kept the engine running and turned the craft to E.S.E. again to prevent her from drifting north again. They dropped anchor to counter the drift of the current and made some coffee, using the hot water they had in the thermos. Harry ate a few digestive biscuits with his but Andrew still felt queasy from the motion of the boat. They prepared the fishing lines and let two of them out over the side. They secured the rods to the fasteners on deck and waited for a bite. It was then 12.30 so they had plenty of time. Occasionally the silhouette of a cargo boat or an oil tanker passed on the horizon, and twice they saw a fishing boat in the distance, bobbing like a small black blob, but little else. The night was cold and the men were very glad of the oilskin slops they wore over their thick jerseys.

They drank a can of beer each from time to time as they kept their eyes on the fishing lines. In between, they boiled up tea, cupping their hands around the mugs to get them warm. The friends stood in turn below deck in the galley, their faces near the glow of the Calor gas ring. Harry topped up the tank with diesel for fear of it running out, in which event the engine would have to be 'bled' before refilling.

'The fish must have gone to bed, Lucky them!' Andrew said yawning. After an hour of checking the lines they had caught but two cod, one of which was so small they put it back, telling it to grow.

'I wish we'd bought a small net instead,' Andrew commented.

'A net's no fun and we don't want a boatful,' Harry told him.

By 4 o'clock, however, they were satisfied with their catch and each went in turn below deck to get a little 'kip' while the other kept watch, before returning to base. They hadn't realised how tired they would be after a day's work at the port. In fact, the whole week had been hard for Harry.

'I'm glad it's Saturday tomorrow,' Andrew said, yawning again, 'at least we can sleep all the morning.'

'I can't. I have to take mother shopping on Saturday mornings, and I'll have to wait till after lunch when she goes for her rest, too,' he told Andrew.

'You poor bugger!' Andrew said, with some feeling for his friend, and took himself off to his bunk.

Chapter Thirteen

At five thirty, the two friends prepared to get back to the harbour. Harry checked the engine and set the craft into motion, scrutinising the compass while veering to the west, in the direction of Southwold. Andrew, in the meantime, washed the mugs and spoons in cold water and tidied the galley and the cabin. They had eaten little but he still felt below par, due to the unfamiliarity of the craft's motion and an inability to wake properly after Harry had almost knocked him off his bunk trying to bring him to.

'My peepers won't work,' he said, sleepily.

'Then feel about, but get cracking,' Harry told him, getting impatient. 'I'm the one who should be tired, I work harder than you,' he commented.

'Bloody cheek,' Andrew replied. Although he began to feel nervous and apprehensive again about entering the mouth of the Blyth he was nevertheless glad Harry felt livelier than he did. He had confidence that his colleague was competent at handling the old craft.

'The tide should still be making by the time we get to the harbour mouth, the wind's getting up a bit, we don't need that,' Harry said, looking up at the sky again. A few small clouds passed in front of the moon's face.

'It'll be nice to get back on terra ferma and get warm again. My feet are as cold as hell,' Andrew said, frowning.

'Hell's hot,' commented Harry, 'anyway, boots are always cold to wear unless you've got thick oiled wool socks on.'

'Mine aren't oiled wool, I don't think, but they're thick,' *Like you!* Harry thought to himself, mildly surprised at how naïve Andrew was. He knew Susan was a good sailor. Andrew had told him how she knew the harbour, having sailed a dinghy in her youth. *She'll have to teach Andrew a few things nautical if he's to give her a yacht or even a small sailing dinghy*, he thought.

Andrew put the lines and rods together to keep busy and to give the impression that he was not nervous. Every few minutes he peered towards the coastline hoping to see it as the moon began to fade. Dawn was not yet showing her light in the east. Andrew was not feeling at all well and could not take the beer Harry offered him from the few he had left in the wheel house.

'Make yourself some tea, Old Boy,' Harry suggested, trying to be helpful.

'No thanks,' Andrew managed to mumble before he rushed to the side and vomited into the sea. He sat down, wiped his mouth and eyes, and put his head in his hands.

'You look like a ghost,' Harry commented.

'I wish I was one, I'd float off this bloody floating wood pile we're on,' Andrew said with feeling. Moments later land came into view which put some optimism back into Andrew's gut and some colour back in his cheeks. Thy chugged on riding the waves like a carousel. The wind had backed to the South and clouds appeared in the sky making the early morning even darker.

'It looks like rain,' Harry said.

'Bloody pessimist,' Andrew said.

'Do you swear this much in front of Susan?' Harry said, realising how much Andrew had been swearing.

'No, of course I bloody well don't. Sorry Old Chum. It's the tension,' Andrew apologised. *Wait till they're married, poor Susan,* Harry thought, already irritated by what he felt were Andrew's mental weaknesses.

'Well, calm down, we're all right. The journey's nearly over,' he told Andrew. The lights of Southwold loomed up as they neared the harbour mouth, providing the men with a welcome sight.

'People are getting up. My God! It's later than I thought,' Harry said with some alarm, looking at his watch. 'The tide is already on the turn. The old tub isn't making as fast as she should. This wind doesn't help,' he went on, trying not to sound as worried as he felt in front of Andrew.

As they neared the harbour, Harry steered the boat to W.N.W. for a while to avoid the sand banks and then turned W.S.W. to ride the deep water channel. Already the tide was running fast, ebbing its way past them impatiently as if longing for the freedom of the sea. Andrew was looking helplessly on while Harry began to feel very tired with suppressed nervous energy and from staring into the darkness that still clung over the water. He kept the harbour lights in view.

'Bugger, it's raining now,' Andrew remarked, unnecessarily. Realising from the look on Harry's face he had made another pessimistic comment, Andrew said, 'At least we've got a good catch to show for our efforts.'

Harry wondered just what effort Andrew had actually made on the trip, *not much,* he thought. Harry had taken all the responsibility for steering and navigating. He had not realised how little Andrew knew of seamanship. The water became more and choppier as they rode against the tide. Andrew went below and came up wearing his life jacket.

'Do you want yours?' He asked.

'No, you pessimist,' Harry said, frowning, 'I've got enough clothes on now I can hardly move. You look like the Michelin man.' He glanced back at Andrew, forcing a smile. They came close to the narrow entrance, the high walls each side of them, and Harry guided the *Maggie* through.

'Well done Harry,' Andrew said with great relief as they entered the Blyth. He felt safe and began to relax. 'At least we're not too late and stuck on a sand bank,' he added.

'We're not moving much though,' Harry commented again. He opened the throttle as far as it would go to get the boat to move faster against the strong ebbing tide. At that moment, the engine stalled and Harry swore. The old boat started to drift sideways.

'Christ, come on!' Harry yelled at the engine, as he tried in vain to restart her.

'Oh, my God! We're going backwards!' Andrew shouted in horror.

'I know we bloody are! What the bloody hell's up with this sodding engine,' Harry said in panic. The engine became flooded with oil as he continued trying to get her into motion. 'Throw the bloody anchor for Christ's sake!' he ordered Andrew.

Before Andrew could do so, the wooden groyne on the right of them loomed out of the semi darkness. The men were helpless to do anything to avoid it and the *Maggie* hit the boards with such force her bow on the portside split with a ghastly cracking sound. At the same time, the two men were thrown on their backs onto the deck. Water came surging in. Andrew levered himself to his feet. The boat again hit the groyne, this time the concrete part. He grabbed the side of it and clung with all his might onto an open slat between the sections of the structure. He pulled himself free from the sinking boat. The *Maggie* veered round, and, what was left of her bow faced the estuary again but she continued to be swept backwards with the tide.

Grunting with the effort needed to hold on, his life jacket keeping him above water he peered back at the *Maggie*, yelling in despair to Harry as the craft disappeared out to sea, the cruel waves breaking her up as she went.

Andrew tried desperately to get a grip with his foot in the gap of the section below, the water continually washing over him. He held on with his forearm through the gap, his hands numb with cold and wondered for how long he would be able to maintain this position against the pull of the tide. Breathing heavily he drew himself up and at last found a footing, relieving his arm a little of the strong grip he'd needed to keep himself from following his friend to his fate. He tried to push his knee into the gap, gasping and pulling himself against the groyne with a strength only found in a life over death situation. He stopped to get a breath and then shouted frantically as loudly as he could to get attention, but to no avail. The light was appearing in the sky. Andrew felt he had been in this situation for hours. In fact,

Southwold pier (above) *and beach huts along the promenade* (below)

View along the harbour front (above) *and the Town Hall – where Andrew and Robert received their bravery awards – and the Swan Hotel* (below)

View from the harbour looking towards St Edmund's Church and the lighthouse (above) *and fishermen's huts along the harbour* (below)

Choppy water in the harbour mouth (above) *and the beach where the body was found* (below)

it was merely minutes. In great despair, he shouted again but no one was in hearing distance at all.

The ebb tide seemed to fight to dislodge Andrew from his precarious position as hard as he fought to keep it. It swept over him. His calls were lost in the flow, his strength ebbing like the tide away from him. He shouted again. This time his call was heard, not from the land but from the sea. A fishing boat chugged into view.

'Where the hell did that come from?' one of the crew said, startled.

'God knows, I can't see anyone,' the other said, looking all around him. Andrew, overwhelmed with hope could utter nothing but automatically let go of his grip with his left hand and waved frantically. At the same time, his right hand, numb with cold, slid from its hold. Andrew was swept seaward. The fishing boat came to the entrance and passed him. Spluttering and throwing up water, his arms thrashing, he yelled in desperation.

Looking behind them the astonished fishermen stared for a moment at the yellow blob of Andrew's life jacket before they realised what they were seeing and both yelled, 'OK, Mate, hold on, we're coming.' Having nothing to hold onto Andrew was swept with the tremendous force of the tide out of the sight of the men. They turned their boat round in the little leeway they had and raced full throttle back on the fast flow to find Andrew. By the time they found him in the poor light of the winter morning, he was unconscious. They hauled him aboard with difficulty. His clothes being saturated made him a dead weight.

'He's dead, Mate,' one of the men said, startled.

'Hold on, I don't think he is,' his mate said. He laid Andrew on the deck and put his fingers on Andrew's wrist, searching for his pulse.

'He's alive, but only just. His pulse is hardly there,' he said. He managed to get Andrew's life jacket off and loosen his clothing. He covered Andrew with an old sack and tarpaulin to get some warmth back into his body, while his friend called the emergency rescue team, pulled anchor and steered for the quay as quickly as possible.

As they moored the boat at Southwold the ambulance arrived, transferred Andrew from the boat onto it and sped off to the hospital, leaving the two fisherman shaking their heads and indeed shaking somewhat, all over.

'Let's get a cuppa and get warm before we tackle anything else.' Suggested Bill, one of the rescuers. They left their boat and trudged heavily to the kiosk near the car park. It had just opened.

'You two look glum this morning. It's not like you,' the woman said as she handed them their first brew of the day.

'Yeah, we've just brought in a chap we found floating about in the sea,' Pete said.

'You're joking?' she said, and after a pause added, 'aren't you?', looking at the serious faces of the two fishermen.

'It's true,' Bill confirmed. 'We saw some bits of plank floating by way-out, didn't we Pete, but it was too dark to see much. Perhaps the chap capsized,' he surmised.

'Bloody silly going out on your own at night,' Pete said, 'Assuming he was alone,' he added, as the thought entered his mind.

'Well, we didn't see a sign of any other silly bugger,' Bill replied.

'We'll ring up the sick house later and find out if he's still in the land of the living,' Pete suggested.

'Do you know who it was?' the woman asked.

'No, he didn't leave his card,' Bill said sarcastically.

The two men each washed down a thick ham sandwich with their tea and then wandered down to attend to their boat, really feeling too exhausted to do so. They then made their way up to the 'Fishermen's Rest', for a proper breakfast and to relate their experience to their mates. On the way, they met Reggie going down to the river to await Harry's and Andrew's return.

'Hi chaps! Did you see the old *Maggie* out there?' he asked them.

'No, very few out last night,' Bill said, 'Someone pinched your beautiful craft?' he added, smiling.

'No, I sold her to two chaps from London, they went out last night on their first fishing trip, should be in by now,' he said, looking towards the mouth of the Blyth.

'We picked up one chap out there,' Pete said, his stomach lurching.

'Bloody hell! Is that true? What did he look like?' Reggie asked concerned.

'Dead!' Bill said.

'He was covered in thick clothes, it's a wonder his life jacket held him up,' Pete said, straightening up and rubbing his back.

'He looked about twenty-five,' Bill informed Reggie.

'By himself?' asked Reggie.

'Yeah, didn't have a girlfriend with him,' Bill said. 'What did you do with him?' Reggie asked.

'We threw him back,' Bill began. 'We got him an ambulance

and got him to the hospital. What the hell did you think we'd do with him, you silly bugger,' Bill added, irritated by Reggie's stupid remark.

Reggie walked briskly to the car park and on to the point where the harbour ended, and stared out to sea. He breathed heavily, his chest heaved, and he twisted his hands about in his pockets in anticipation and fear that one of the men was Andrew or Harry. He moved up and down, staring at the water, then at the wooden groyne on the opposite side of the narrow bottleneck of the river entrance, then out to sea, longing for the *Maggie* to put in an appearance. When he suddenly felt cold, he turned inland. He had an idea to ring the hospital to determine who the victim was.

Chapter Fourteen

ndrew was suffering from hypothermia in the hospital and had not gained consciousness by the time Reggie telephoned there, so he could not get his name. Greatly worried by this time, Reggie slipped out of The Lord Nelson, made his way miserably to the James Paget hospital, and asked to see the patient rescued from the sea.

'It's not possible yet, the doctor is with him. Are you a relative?' the casualty nurse asked.

'No, a friend, I think,' Reggie said, feeling a little stupid, not really knowing who the victim was.

'Then I'm afraid you will have to telephone later,' she informed him. Reggie, feeling frustrated, went back to the pub to see if Pete and Bill were still there, but they had gone. He drank down half pint of Adnams and biked back to the harbour. A little ray of hope came into his mind that perhaps the two men had left the fishing grounds too late, the boat had been stuck on a sand bank, and they were waiting for the next tide to bring them in. He screwed up his eyes, looking towards the eastern horizon but saw nothing. The ray of hope left him. The wind blew strongly, full daylight appeared, but still he waited, unable to believe the tragedy had happened.

Meanwhile, Harry's mother also waited. She glanced frequently at the telephone willing it to ring. The hands of the clock moved round, slowly it seemed, to eight o'clock, then to nine and still no communication from her son. Eventually, at ten o'clock, she rang the police but they could tell her nothing. *Perhaps they decided to stay out fishing longer*, Betty told herself, but in her heart she knew Harry would realise she would worry and would not do that. At twenty to elven the doorbell rang and with a mixture of joy and anticipation, she hurried to the door, *perhaps Harry had forgotten his key*, she thought. She opened the door. Her heart missed a beat. She gripped the doorknob tightly. A policeman and policewoman stood there.

'Are you Mrs Redford?' the young man asked.

'Yes, why, what's happened?' Betty stammered.

'May we come in please? I'm afraid we have some bad news,' he said, edging his way in. Betty put her hand to her mouth in fear, unable to speak.

'We're afraid it's your son, Mrs Redford. He's been lost at sea. His boat sank early this morning,' the policeman told her. The woman put her arm around Betty who began to sob quietly, looking in disbelief, from them, to the floor and shaking her head. She turned pale, put her hand to her head, feeling dizzy, and for a moment seemed to pass out. The policeman ran to get a chair while the woman tried to support her. He slipped the seat under her and they both held her there, putting her head between her knees and massaging the back of her neck. She came round, lifted her head, and looked at them pitiably and through renewed sobs said, 'No, it can't be.' Eventually she asked, 'And his friend Andrew, has he gone too?'

'No, he was picked up, but he's in a bad state. He's in hospital,' they told Betty.

'Did he say what happened?' she asked.

'He was unconscious when he arrived there, but our colleagues are with him now. All we know at present is that he asked us to tell you and to give you his commiserations,' Betty heard through her aura of misery.

'Have they found my Boy?' she asked, looking from one to another.

'No, his friend was unconscious for some time after they brought him in, there seems little hope, I'm afraid. He's too exhausted and upset to talk much and time is against us,' the policeman told her.

'But they are doing their best,' the police woman said, trying to comfort Betty. 'May I make you a tea? I think we all could do with a cup,' she tried to smile. Betty stood up, holding onto the girl's arm and they went into the kitchen where Betty sat down and pointed to the tea pot and caddy.

'What is your name dear?' She asked at last.

'Jean, my Dear. Here let me help you to drink this,' she said after pouring out the tea. Jean held the cup to Betty's mouth while she sipped the hot, sweet tea, shaking almost too much to drink. The policeman said he'd keep in touch and let her know of any news and left Jean there to comfort her while he returned to base.

Andrew was put in a side ward and monitored every half hour to get his body temperature gradually back to normal.

After nearly ten hours, he regained consciousness. Propped up in bed, he re-lived the ghastly nightmare he had experienced but hours before. He was too weak to ring Susan and decided it best to contact her after work at her flat, when he might feel stronger. He wanted her to know before her parents heard. Desperately sad, he tried to sleep to forget the trauma of the night before. He felt somewhat culpable at having persuaded Harry to buy such an old boat, and indeed, at having got him involved at all. He buried his face under the covers and wept till sleep overcame him.

When he awoke three hours later, Susan was sitting by his bed, holding his hand. He looked worn and confused, peering round the room and wondering where he was. When he saw her, tears welled up in their eyes simultaneously and she squeezed his hand.

'My Love, my Love. Thank goodness you're all right,' her words were mixed with sobs, and half smiles of joy.

'Harry isn't. He's gone, it was dreadful,' he said, his mouth quivering.

'Don't tell me now, you must rest, Darling,' she told him and held the back of his hand against her wet cheek.

'My arms ache like hell and my throat is sore,' Andrew told her, frowning.

'I'll get the nurse to give you some more painkillers. I expect you swallowed a lot of salt water,' Susan said, releasing his hand and standing up. She wiped the tears from her eyes and face, and went to find a nurse. When the male nurse returned with Susan, he advised her to leave Andrew for a while so that he could rest completely. He gave him a sleeping tablet, which Andrew felt he hardly needed, being already utterly exhausted after his ordeal. The nurse offered Susan a bed in the visitor's room kept for patient's families, but she told him that her parents lived in Southwold. They had rung her just after she had arrived late home from work, having heard the news on Anglia television, at 6.25pm, and had been greatly surprised and shocked to hear Andrew's name mentioned. The police had been at the hospital waiting to interview him but had left, finding him in no state to communicate. The Press had also attempted to make contact, so the television announcement had been brief.

Susan had gathered some clothes together and sped up the A12 to the James Paget straight away, her heart heavy with anxiety. Bob and Jill had met her in the hospital foyer and waited there for Susan to re-appear from being with Andrew to tell them the latest news. Susan, at that point could tell them little except that Andrew was going to be all right. They drove back to the house in their separate cars and prepared food for themselves, though no one really felt like eating.

After Susan had rung the ward to hear that Andrew was sleeping soundly, Bob poured them all a strong whisky and Susan's mother tucked her up in bed and stayed with her a while as she had done at troubled times when Susan was a child. Her parents retired to bed, themselves suffering from the dreadful realisation of what the loss of his friend would mean to Andrew.

'We are lucky that Andrew is still with us,' Jill commented, as they lay awake, unable to sleep. Like Andrew, Susan cried herself to sleep thinking how sad that his friend was gone, and at the same time grateful Andrew had been saved.

Chapter Fifteen

The next day the police arrived at the hospital to take a detailed statement, which Andrew had been unable to give them the day before. He had woken early feeling much better physically but, being more aware, felt much worse emotionally. His thoughts of the fishing trip went round and round in his head and by the time the police officer came, he had a clearer picture of what to tell them.

Susan had rung and learned that Andrew was much improved. When she learned that the police were interviewing Andrew she sent a message of love and support to him and was told she could ring later and find out when it was possible to visit him.

Andrew asked the police for news of Harry's mother and was told her sister had taken Betty to her home so that she would not be in the house alone. Harry had always been at home with his mother, being a bachelor still. His father had died nine years previously, and so Betty never lived alone. She had taken her only child's death badly as was to be expected, the police told Andrew, who was already aware of that.

Susan stayed in bed until after breakfast. Her mother took it up to her on a tray so that she could rest and be on her own for a while. She did not feel like talking, she told Jill, who sympathised. The night had seemed long and Susan, like her parents, had not slept much, which left her very tired.

Andrew was also very tired by the time the police had left, in fact, he felt utterly exhausted. They had asked him so many questions. He turned these, and the answers he had given them, repeatedly in his mind. He felt like they were interrogating him at times but realised they were simply looking for the truth. They had to determine that Harry had died accidentally, and wanted to know the full event leading to his death.

When Susan returned to his ward at half past eleven, she was disappointed to find him in a deep sleep again. She went off to the café and drank coffee while she read the latest edition of 'Ideal Home' magazine she had bought in the hospital foyer. She could not face reading the newspapers. She cheered herself up by looking at materials and getting ideas for furnishings for their new home. How relieved she was to realise her fiancé had survived, due, she knew to the fact that he had worn a life jacket. 'If only Harry had worn one. I offered it to him but he refused,' Susan remembered Andrew telling her in despair. When she got back to the ward, Andrew was awake and trying to eat some lunch. He waved to her with his fork as he saw her come through the door. She was overjoyed to see him with some colour in his cheeks and bent to kiss them.

'You look as tired as I feel, Darling,' he said, scrutinising her face.

'None of us slept very well, thinking mostly of what could have happened to you. Poor Harry isn't suffering anymore but his poor mother must be in a terrible state,' Susan said.

'I can't eat anymore,' Andrew said, pushing his plate down the bed. He wished Susan had not mentioned Harry's mother. The thought of her misery made him feel the same and he immediately lost what little appetite he had.

'Mummy rang Robert last night to tell him the news. He sent his best wishes to you, and was sorry to hear about Harry,' Susan said. She did not mention that Robert had said he was not surprised if they went out in the old boat he saw them in.

'Thanks, I'll look forward to seeing him at our wedding, I hope he will be able to get the time off to come to it,' Andrew said, lying back on the pillow.

'I've been looking through this mag,' Susan said, opening the page showing Liberty materials, hoping to divert his attention from the fate of his friend, 'I'm longing to choose the wall paper and curtains for our flat, with you,' she said, smiling and taking his hand.

'Perhaps it will be done already. The last people might leave theirs behind,' he said, teasing her.

'Then it'll all go,' Susan told him, in a determined voice, just in case he meant it.

Andrew was kept in hospital for another three days just in case he developed an adverse reaction caused by the shock his mind and body had undergone. When he came out, he was invited to spend the rest of the week at Jill and Bob's home. They looked after him very well while Susan returned to work on the Wednesday, and came home again Friday evening. He borrowed pyjamas and some day clothes from Bob, which amused Susan when he greeted her at the door on her arrival home.

'A bit big for you, Darling, or have you lost a lot of weight?' she laughed.

'Wait till you see me in your Pa's pyjamas,' he smiled, putting his arm around her shoulder as they walked back in from the car.

'I hope I shan't,' she said emphatically, 'It might put me off you,' she added, trying to look serious.

The family went out to dinner at The Swan Hotel that night and spent the rest of the weekend together trying to enjoy moments when Andrew's mind was not pre occupied with the horrors of the previous weekend. They went for a walk on the bright, but cold Sunday, taking care to venture in the opposite direction from the harbour. Susan cast a sideways glance at Andrew's expression from time to time and wondered how long it would take him to get the desperately sad look and feeling of loss out of his system. *Never, entirely, of course,* she told herself. Sometimes she noticed him shiver slightly and realised he was still suffering from shock.

They did not stay out for long and spent the rest of the weekend trying to relax by the warm log fire. Bob gave Andrew a few books by Frederick Forsyth and Wilbur Smith but either he had read them already or couldn't concentrate for long enough to read much. Mostly he put his head back on the sofa, where he sat with Susan, holding her hand, and pretended to be asleep. *No one, not even Sue, can know what I think and feel,* he thought to himself. He decided to return to his flat on the Monday to enable him to gather his thoughts together on his own and try to come to terms with his life without his friend Harry.

Andrew asked Susan to collect his car from Walberswick before darkness fell on Sunday afternoon and gave her the set of keys, which, luckily, had remained secure, zipped in his wet anorak pocket and had been recovered when Jill washed the clothes Susan had brought back from hospital. He could not face returning to that scene which earlier had held such hope and excitement for him. Jill and Bob drove Susan the eight miles round to Walberswick to collect the car. It was too cold to walk the mile down the harbour and across the footbridge. While they were gone, Andrew rested by the fire still and thought how lucky he was, not only to be alive, but also to have a nice family to love for the first time in his life. He began to realise that this was more precious than being rich.

The next morning Susan had to leave early to get back to London to work. She was unable to take more time off as Christmas was almost upon them. She crept into Robert's room to say goodbye to Andrew. They held each other tightly and kissed but she persuaded him to stay in bed longer and not get up to see her off. They planned to meet the next day when he had sorted himself out at home but would talk to each other on the phone that evening when Susan got back to her flat.

'I shall be glad when we're married so we can be together every night,' she told Andrew.

'It's not long now, my Love,' he said, smiling.

Susan thanked her parents for all they had done for Andrew. Her mother waved from the window while Bob put his coat on over his dressing gown as the early morning felt very cold indeed.

'Poor old Susan, having to leave at this ungodly hour,' Jill said, glad that her days of going out to work were over. *Enough to cope with here*, she thought.

Andrew got up and went downstairs to breakfast just as Jill and Bob were finishing theirs. He apologised but felt better about it when he saw that Bob was still in his pyjamas and dressing gown. He seldom got to the office before 10am, and only had to get to the town. Sometimes, weather permitting, he even walked.

Chapter Sixteen

Just after the New Year, when Andrew was back at work, he received, one evening on reaching home, a brown envelope amongst his mail marked 'Private and Confidential'. He stood in the hall and fingered it gingerly fearing it might be bad news. Slitting it open, he glanced rapidly down the page. His hands began to shake. He sighed and tears of relief welled up so that he could hardly re-read the news. He sat down on the bottom of the stairs in the entrance hall to the flats. He wiped the tears away and re-read the words, hardly able to take in their contents.

A smile spread across his face. He put his head in his hands, as if to help his brain to take in what he had read. Then he jumped up and ran up to his flat two stairs at a time. He fumbled with his key, let himself in and slamming the door behind him, strode to the telephone and flopped into his armchair. Having recovered his breath, he dialled Susan's number at home. No answer. He dialled her work number to find she had just left. He paced up and down the room with a whisky in one hand and the letter in the other. He kept looking at it as if he was afraid it would disappear.

After several impatient tries, Andrew at last heard Susan's

voice on the other end of the phone.

'Hello Darling, I've only just got in,' she told him.

'I know. I've rung you at work and several times at home.'

'Is anything wrong? You sound flustered,' Susan asked.

'Darling, I've been awarded a medal for bravery! Can you imagine that?!' he told her

'Goodness! No, I can't. What for, being rescued?' she asked, without thinking further.

'You silly thing, it's for rescuing that kid.'

Good heavens! How incredible,' she said, not meaning to sound disparaging, 'who initiated that?'

'The Boy's mother and the ambulance men apparently. Listen, I'll read it out to you,'

'I wonder if Robert will get one,' Susan said after listening to Andrew reading the letter to her.

'He deserves it too,' Andrew agreed.

'I'll ring home to see if they've heard anything,' she said.

They talked for a while and Susan became as excited as Andrew.

'I wonder who's going to present it to you and where?' she asked.

'They're going to let me know,' Andrew repeated to her glancing down the page again. Jill and Bob knew nothing of the award so were surprised when Susan rang them. They sent their congratulations to Andrew via her.

'Robert ought to get a medal too, he was just as brave,' said Jill.

'Yes, he resuscitated the little lad,' Bob said.

'I wonder if they will send it here or Aldershot if he does get one.'

'Let's ring him. We can tell him about Andrew, at least.' Jill suggested.

'Better wait till tomorrow and see if anything comes in the post,' Bill said, sitting down in his armchair.

Next morning Jill was up early waiting for the postman, but nothing came for Robert. Twice she flitted through the mail before handing it to Bob as he came downstairs in his dressing gown and slippers.

'We'll ring him tonight anyway,' Jill said, feeling impatient and wanting an excuse to talk to her son. 'He will be pleased for Andrew, I'm sure.'

As soon as 6 o'clock came round that evening, Jill got through to Robert.

'Hello, Ma! What makes you ring so soon?' he asked, hearing his mother's voice for the second time since New Year. 'No more bad news is it? How's Andrew?'

'He's much better, back at work. He's won a medal for bravery.'

'What the hell for?' Robert asked, surprised.

'For pulling that little boy out of the sea. We hoped you'd get one. You deserve it too Son, you saved his life after Andrew rescued him,' his mother went on.

'Andrew did the hardest part. The water was so cold, and rough, I wonder that he didn't drown with the boy. I am jolly glad for his sake, especially after the awful ordeal he's been through and losing his best friend, poor devil. That old fisherman ought to be sued for selling them that clapped out old boat, if it was the one that John and I saw him on that day,' Robert remembered. 'Anyway,' he went on, 'it will give Andrew a big boost and please

Susan as well. Congratulate him for me, Ma,' Robert then chatted to his father for a few minutes, telling him he might be home in two weeks for a few days, but not to mention it to Jill in case it did not come off.

'OK, take care of yourself, my Boy, bye for now,' and Bob put the phone on the hook smiling to himself and, feeling elated, poured a whisky for himself and a gin and tonic for his wife.

To the delight of both his parents, a brown envelope arrived for Robert the next morning. It had 'Personal and Confidential' printed on the top left hand corner so they guessed it might be what they were hoping for. Jill fumbled with it, with all her fingers longing to tear it open. She wanted to ring Robert there and then to ask if she may do so. However, they knew Robert would not be in the mess until later or the office, so were compelled to wait until the evening and hoped he would be back in camp. During the day when Bob was not in the hall, Jill kept picking up the envelope as if by some chance it would reveal its contents. At 6 o'clock sharp, she dialled the number excitedly as she had done two nights before but was told Robert was not in the mess. Whoever answered offered to try to locate him. Jill stood first on one foot and then the other impatiently and biting her top lip in anticipation. At last she was told Robert could not be found, so, disappointed, she left a message asking Robert to contact them when he got in

'I can't bear the suspense,' she told Bob, walking up and down in the lounge.

'For goodness sakes, sit down. You look like something you see in the zoo, pacing its cage,' Bob said, looking up from his book.

'You're so casual, Darling, how can you switch off? I have been waiting for this moment all day. I hope he returns from his cross country or wherever it is they go,' she said, flopping down into the chair reluctantly.

'Anyone would think he'd won the lottery. The letter might not be anything important. He's had mail coming here before now,' he sighed, resting his book on his lap, unable to concentrate on the story.

Twenty minutes later, the phone rang. Jill jumped up and ran to pick it up as if afraid it would elude her.

'Hi, Mum, what now?' Robert asked, abruptly, in anticipation of more bad news. His parents had never rung him so often.

'Nothing, Darling, only there's an envelope that's arrived for you and we think it might be important.' She now felt rather silly as they usually sent mail onto him as soon as it arrived.

'I know you're longing to open it. It can't be so important that my Mother shouldn't read it, unless I've been a naughty boy and the police are after me.' Robert said, trying to humour her to cover up his impatience.

'Hold on, I'll put the phone down a moment.' Jill tore open the brown envelope nervously, hoping it would contain the good news she wanted to read.

'As I thought!' she shrieked. She grabbed the phone, spoke to Robert into the ear piece, turned it round and yelled to him, 'You've got one too, well done, Darling!'

'Got what, Ma?' he asked, guessing himself what it was.

'A bravery medal, like Andrew. I knew it was. All day I've felt it in my bones,' she told him, unable to stand still. 'Here's your Father, Bye Son,' Jill handed the phone to Bob and went into the lounge feeling a little deflated... His father congratulated Robert, after which he was glad to get off the phone. He walked slowly to the bar and ordered a brandy. He felt elated but tried to suppress his pride. He hoped that if he got leave in two weeks it would coincide with receiving his medal at the same time that Andrew received his.

Chapter Seventeen

*J*ill rang her daughter that same evening to tell her of Robert's award.

'How super, two in one family! I hope Rob can get home for the presentation. Let me know where and when it is or if I hear first from Andrew I will ring and let you know straight away. In the meantime I'll ring the Boy's mother and the ambulance men to thank them.' Susan said.

'She sounds more excited by it than Robert did,' Jill said, looking at Bob.

'Men don't get excited and het up about these things, we're less hedonistic than you women,' he replied, putting his nose in the air and smiling.

'Huh! You men go about your pleasures in a quieter way, secretive and less open. Understandable, considering some of the pleasures you get up to,' she said.

'Chance would be a fine thing, Darling,' he pretended to pout.

'Yes, I can imagine, in your case,' Jill said, looking him up and down and pretending to sneer, 'Though you've had enough tarty secretaries through your fingers in your time,'

'Not literally, and I object to you calling them tarts. They were all very respectable,' he protested.

'Sorry Darling, I admit I've never had to feel the least bit jealous of the ones I've met!'

'Come here, you Honey. Why would I want to look at another woman when I have you,' Bob said, grabbing her around the waist.

'Now what do you want to borrow?' she asked, glancing up into his face.

'You, please! Come on, I want to make love to you.' She put her face to his and they kissed long while he stroked her buttocks with both hands. He pressed her to him. She broke away from him, and went into the hall. He followed. She set the answer phone, and then took his hand. They looked at each other and smiled. She led him upstairs.

The presentation ceremony was arranged to be held at the Town Hall. Having confirmed that his leave would definitely be on the 3rd of February, Robert informed his parents, who in turn told the Town Clerk. The room was booked for the Friday evening, allowing Susan and Andrew to be there. At 7pm on that day, a small group of proud people assembled in a room at the Town Hall. Susan had invited Alison Harrison and her small son Johnny, who now looked fit and had grown since thy last saw him. Susan had kindly thought to buy him a large red football. He took it, shyly smiling. She thought Alison looked shy too, and turned to put her arm around her shoulder.

'It was good of you to do this Alison,' she smiled.

'It was the least I could do, without them my Johnny wouldn't be here.' She said, trying to smile but almost crying.

The medals were pinned on Andrew's and Robert's lapels while Bob, Jill and Susan watched in admiration. They were pleasantly surprised that the two men who had rescued Andrew were there as well and receiving medals. The Mayor made a small speech. Jill wiped her eyes and Bob squeezed her hand. After handshakes, congratulations, and thanks all round, the press took notes and family photographs were taken. The ambulance representative, one of the crew who had taken Johnny to the hospital, left with Alison and her son, giving them a lift home. Andrew thanked his two rescuers.

'Now we'll go and celebrate over dinner at the 'Swan',' Bob told them.

'Oh goody! I love going there, it's a big treat,' Susan smiled.

'All meals are a treat for you, Greedy Guts!' her brother said, striding out in front.

'You look in a hurry yourself, old chap,' Bob said.

The merry party sat down at a table Bob had already booked for them secretly during the day. They raised their glasses of champagne to the two heroes who both felt somewhat embarrassed in the presence of a restaurant full of people, some of whom joined in the cheers, not knowing why until one of them asked. Of course then they wished to see the medals which embarrassed the men even further. Andrew still had his pinned to his lapel but Robert had taken his off and put it in his pocket.

'Thank the Lord that's over,' he said, as he walked through the door of his parents' home.

'Well, we may as well finish the day with our private little celebration,' Bob suggested, going to the sideboard and getting out the drinks.

'Yes, good idea, Darling,' Jill said, flopping into Bob's armchair.

'And you can get your bottom out of that. It's mine,' Bob smiled, turning his head to look at her. She got up, picked up a cushion and was about to throw it at him, when Robert intervened and snatched it away from her.

'Spoil sport,' she said, wobbling over to her usual chair.

'You're tipsy already, Ma. Give her some Alka-Seltzer Dad!' Robert advised.

Bob smiled and handed his wife a very weak gin and tonic, she sipped it.

'What do you call this?' she emphasised 'do'.

'I have to keep you under control, my Love,' Bob told her.

Susan looked at Andrew, and smiled. *Till later* she thought, but said, 'Really, you two act like children when you've had a drink.'

'Listen to Grandma talking!' Andrew laughed, squeezing her hand.

The party quietened down suddenly, fatigue overcoming them from the evening's excitement and the excess of rich food and drink. Bob put on a tape recording of Mozart's Horn Concerto and they all sipped their drinks and listened to it, glad they did not have to make conversation. Eventually Jill got up, swinging her hips to give the impression she was in control of her body, made a crooked routine to the kitchen. She put the kettle on and called above Mozart,

'Anyone for a coffee?' the response was a mixed chorus of, 'Yes, please', and 'No, thank you'. Susan jumped up and swept to the kitchen on air, it seemed to her. She got out the cups, saying, 'Three coffees and one tea, and whatever you want, Mum.' They made the drinks, and took them in, one or two overflowing onto the saucers. The men looked at each other with raised eyebrows and smiled, but said nothing.

Mozart ended his Concerto and the family prepared for bed. Bob and Jill were the last going up. He took her arm to support her and led her to their room.

'You're not used to it, are you old thing?' he smiled as she flopped onto the bed.'

'I beg your pardon! Not used to what, may I ask? And not so much of the 'old', you're older than I am!' Jill waffled on, slurring her words. Bob helped her to prepare for bed after which she fell into a deep sleep, snoring gently. Bob smiled to himself and turned over.

Susan waited until all was quiet and slipped into Andrew's room. She jumped into bed and he took her into his arms.

'Hello, my Darling, my hero,' she said, stroking his hair. He smiled and said nothing, then took her head in his hands and kissed her passionately. They made love and lay back in each other's arms and fell asleep.

Susan woke at about 4am, glanced at her sleeping lover, and crept to the bathroom. On her way back to her own bed, her father came out of his room and their eyes met. She felt her face flush but Bob smiled and put a finger to his lips, indicating to her that his discovery would remain a secret. A pang of jealousy swept through him all the same, a natural reaction of a father to his little girl growing up. Susan blew him a kiss, and slipping into her room, quietly closed the door. She got into her cold bed and lay for some time thinking of the day's events, smiling to herself. She felt so happy, appreciating her family as well as being so in love with Andrew.

The next day, the evening paper held a good photograph of Andrew and Robert standing with Alison and little Johnny, holding tightly to his new football. The caption read; 'BRAVERY AWARDS FOR SEA RESCUE,' and went on to describe the events that saved Johnny's life.

'Look at that, isn't that something! We are so proud of you both,' Jill held the paper at arm's length while she expressed her delight.

'Oh God! I shan't go into town for a day or two, I might be recognised,' Robert moaned.

'Go on, you should be proud of yourself, and Andrew too,' she added hastily.

Robert said nothing and Andrew just smiled.

Days later both men were glad to be back at work, especially Robert, who had had to contend with his mother's proud enthusiasm when on the phone to all their relatives and friends everywhere. She went out and had as many as a dozen copies made of the newspaper cutting to send off either to all who asked for them, or to whom she offered them. She was rather indignant that the national press had not got hold of the story and wanted to phone one or two until Bob informed her that it would be of no interest to people outside the Southwold area.

Robert was tremendously put out when he arrived back at his camp and was greeted by cheers and enthusiastic congratulations from all in the mess and even elsewhere. He learned that his father had forwarded a copy of the article to his Commandant. He thought his mother was quite capable of doing this but not his father. He wrote and told them so in anger, which left them with a feeling of depressed anti-climax for a few days.

'Who said he wouldn't mind if I sent it?' Bob said, looking at Jill accusingly.

'He'll never make a really strong officer. He's too modest, not arrogant enough,' Jill frowned.

'I'd rather have him as he is, never the less,' Bob concluded.

Chapter Eighteen

March came and Susan spent much time preparing for her wedding. She was naturally becoming more and more excited about the prospect, buying clothes to go away in which she did not want to show Andrew till she had them on and selecting her wedding dress in the company of her mother, she decided on an off white one with a low neck, tight bodice and long sleeves with small button's along the cuff. Her friend lent her a long petticoat, and Susan bought some pretty blue briefs. 'Something old, something new, something borrowed and something blue,' she reminded herself, deciding to wear an old bra to complete the outfit.

Andrew seemed far less enthusiastic about their impending event. Susan concluded that men don't get excited about things, not even their own weddings. Just a bit nervous perhaps. She mentioned this to her mother one afternoon after shopping in the West End whilst taking tea at Fortnum & Mason's.

'It's quite right, they don't, Dear. Bob told me, as if I didn't already know, only about a month or so ago. In fact at the Boys' presentation,' she added, 'I do think perhaps the terrible tragedy of losing his friend and being rescued himself has taken its toll.

One doesn't really know how he feels inside. He doesn't mention it much, does he?' she turned the last comment into a question.

'No, and I refrain from bringing it up in conversation. I want him to forget it. I suppose I'm protecting myself as much as Andrew to be honest. I don't like thinking about morbid things. Selfish really,' she thought aloud.

Jill squeezed Susan's hand. 'Its best. You've got to think of your great day and life together. You are quite sure this is what you want, isn't it, my Love?'

'Oh gosh, yes! No doubt whatsoever. I'm looking forward to being a housewife,' Susan smiled, looking at her mother.

'That's the drudge part of being married, but nowadays the men do their fair share. You are going to carry on working aren't you, Darling? Jill asked.

'Yes, of course, until we have children,' Susan flushed and turned her hankie round and round in her hand. She stretched herself discreetly, wanting to end the questioning by her mother and leave the building. She insisted on paying the bill, which gave her an excuse to leave her seat. They left the shop and Susan hailed a taxi for her mother to go to Liverpool Street to catch her train home.

'Bye, Darling, thanks for the tea. It's been fun. Shall we see you at the weekend?' Jill asked hopefully.

'I doubt it, Mum, I've lots to do at the flat before the wedding. I've got to find a space for Andrew's things till we find a bigger place.' Susan told her. She waved her mother off in the taxi and caught the underground at Piccadilly Circus to go home. She sat looking down at her parcels feeling uneasy. Her thoughts moved to her wardrobe and drawers and to the mess they were in, through all the preparations she had to make, and through her imaginings of herself on her wedding day. Her mother did the same whilst sitting on the train, only her thoughts went through the food preparations for the day before the wedding, through the outfit she would wear and through worries of her daughter's future happiness.

It was certainly true that Andrew was feeling the loss of his close friend Harry. He had nightmares about struggling in water, about reaching out to grab something as he was sinking, sometimes in water but sometimes in quick sand and even falling out of the sky. He dreamed of the boat and Harry reaching into the water over the side, of himself being shut in the cabin or sometimes in a dark room and not being able to find the door, groping his way along the rough wall. All these dreams and many more disturbed his sleep and so, during the day, he fought to concentrate on his work.

Susan knew nothing of all this but worried about him when he came to her flat dead tired, sometimes too tired to make love, even. She fed him well and showed patience when he had not listened to what she had said. She made excuses for him, remembering what her mother had said about delayed reactions and hoped it was nothing more.

'You're not having second thoughts about our marriage are you, Darling?' she ventured to ask one evening when they sat on the sofa together after their meal.

'No, of course not, why do you ask, Love?' Andrew enquired, looking into her face.

'It's just that you look so tired these days. Are you worried about something?' Susan had tried to broach the question for some time and had only now found the courage.

'No, not really. A few difficulties at work, nothing for you to trouble your head about,' Andrew tried to sound casual and to change the subject, but Susan went on.

'You're not going to be made redundant or anything, are you?' she asked him.

'No, that's out of the question, especially now Harry's gone. There's more to do till they advertise his job,' Andrew said, with pain in his heart and on his face. He wanted to leave and go home to be alone with his thoughts. He disliked being asked questions connected with his friend. He felt somewhat responsible for Harry's death. He jumped up and offered to make coffee, which Susan let him do while she sat looking at the electric fire hoping the excitement would soon return to their lives and make them happy. Andrew left Susan's flat at 11.30pm and she took herself off to bed feeling ill at ease at having asked him which she had previously resolved not to do. She lay awake feeling miserable and slept fitfully.

Chapter Nineteen

'What the hell's that, Barry?'

'Looks like a seal,' Barry Morgan shouted back, peering down to the shore line to where his friend Martin Hall was looking. Both men walked down to get a better view carrying their metal detectors with them. Neither man spoke for a full minute, but stared in disbelief, unable to take in the sight they beheld. They backed away simultaneously.

'Christ!' Barry exclaimed with emphasis, unable to take his eyes away from what he saw.

'It's a fellow, I think. My God! Run Boy, we must get to the police.'

The two men ran up the beach as fast as they could, both feeling physically sick. Martin stopped, put down his metal detector, and looked through his binoculars at the coast guard lookout.

'No one there, we'll make for the 'Red Lion,' he panted, knowing the police station was at the end of the High Street.

'Makes you feel weak at the knees. I wonder who the hell it was,' Barry muttered.

The two men breathlessly pushed past the crowd in the pub

to the telephone. They knew where to find it. Barry dialled 999, his hand shaking.

'What's going on?' the proprietor asked, over Martin's shoulder.

He then heard Barry explain what the urgency was. In fact, most of the customers heard. Eyebrows were raised. A sudden volume of excited muttering took place. A number of morbidly interested men left to go and investigate. Martin and Barry followed them out of the inn and waited a short time before the police arrived.

'Where did you see the body?' one of them asked. Before they could utter a word in reply his other two colleagues jumped out of the car and ushered Barry and Martin in the back away from the gaping crowds who had emptied the bar.

The driver got in and they sped the short way, past South Green Lodge to the path leading down to the promenade. A small crowd had gathered.

'You stay here, Richard, and take some statements. Stay where you are, in the warm,' the senior police sergeant told Barry and Martin. The two men had no desire to venture down to the shore again, anyway. They sat in the car with Richard, suffering from shock and gave an account of who they were, why they were down there and what they saw, shuddering at the last piece of information. They both wondered how the policemen of this world manage to cope and contend with ghastly sights and jobs like this one. They didn't even look down to the beach to see what the men were doing at that point in time, unlike some of the chaps from the pub who were standing on the promenade, some with their hands in their pockets nonchalantly.

They've probably seen worse in their time, or else they're putting on a front to make themselves look tough, thought Barry.

At that moment more police arrived and cleared the promenade of people, a few of them women, Martin and Barry were appalled to notice. A low ambulance arrived and the body was brought up wrapped in a black tarpaulin looking sling and placed in the vehicle. It drove off in haste and the people dispersed. Barry and Martin were driven to the police station to be asked for identification and addresses.

Next day at work Andrew felt that the staff there were avoiding him altogether, through embarrassment, not knowing what to say, or because they blamed Andrew for what had happened. He could not tell which. At times, he did feel that fingers were being pointed at him, poking into the very centre of the guilt cells of his brain. The papers showed pictures of the two men who had found the body but at the time identification had not been established. He went home in a confused daze of misery, not knowing if his friend had actually been washed up on that beach after so long or not. He paced up and down in his lounge, drank a glass of whisky too quickly, picked up the telephone and placed it back on its receiver three times, looked at his screwed up pale face in the mirror, picked up Susan's picture that he'd taken of her and flopped down in the chair, covering his ears with his hands, as if he did not want to hear anything to do with life, let alone death.

He jumped up. The telephone was ringing. He felt unready to talk to anyone, but gingerly picked up the receiver.

'Hello! Who's that?' Andrew asked abruptly before the caller could tell him.

'Hello Darling! Have you seen today's paper?' before she needed to go on Andrew confirmed that he had.

'They don't know if it's him or not yet, do they?'

'No,' he answered dully.

'Are you all right, my Love? You sound tired, still,' Susan went on, feeling anxious about him, yet irritated he was making no effort. Andrew's doorbell rang.

'Listen Honey, I'll have to go, someone at the door. I will ring you tomorrow. I love you,' he added, to cheer her before putting down the phone. Susan felt little cheer, even with that remark from her fiancé. *Another evening spoilt,* she thought, and rang a girl-friend to forget her troubled mind.

The doorbell rang again just as Andrew got there. He opened the door to find two police men filling the entrance.

'Mr Denby?' one asked before Andrew had chance to speak.

'Yes, come in,' they were half inside before he had finished.

'We'd like you to come with us to the station.'

'Now, so late?' Andrew interrupted wearily, his heart beating fast all the same.

'I'm afraid so, you might be able to help us with some inquiries,'

'Concerning what?' Andrew asked, though guessing it would be to do with Harry. He put on his overcoat and locked the door of his flat behind them. The officers said nothing until they got into the car.

'What's this to do with?' Andrew asked again, fearful of the reply. He stuffed his hands in his pockets and stretched out his legs in the back of the car beside one of the police officers, to give an air of nonchalance. His insides were far from composed.

'It's to do with a body that was washed up on Southwold beach, yesterday. You might have seen it in the press,' the constable, who was driving, glancing through the mirror at Andrew whilst Andrew saw the other one next to him staring at him. He thought for a moment.

'D'you think it might be my friend who was drowned in January?' he asked. 'I hope it is, especially for his mother's sake'.

'Perhaps, we're not sure yet,' beyond that, the police were non-committal. Nothing more was said as the car sped along Chigwell High Road to the police station. The men got out and entered the building. Andrew's heart pounded. He was guided into a room where the police detective questioned him who had been bought in for the case.

Andrew was deeply shocked to be told the police wanted him to travel with them to Southwold early the next morning to try to identify the body.

'My God! Do I really have to do that? What if I refuse?' he mumbled, his head swimming.

'I'm afraid you will have no option, Sir,' the detective told him, picking up the phone. He asked the telephonist on site to get him the Southwold Station. Andrew heard him tell them that he was with them and after a few 'OK's' the detective put the phone down and informed Andrew they wanted him up there immediately.

'Christ! Don't you chap's sleep? Surely to God they're not expecting me to do that job tonight?' he moaned incredulously.

'No, I'm sure they won't, but they want to ask you a few questions before then. Here, this'll keep you awake,' the inspector told him as he handed Andrew a mug of hot coffee, which

Andrew held with both hands, gaining some small solace from its warmth. He drank the contents slowly. They then ushered him out into the cold night and opened the car door for him to get in. Utterly miserable and somewhat frightened, Andrew huddled in the back and said nothing during most of the long drive. In fact, in odd moments he found himself nodding off in a muddle headed doze despite his fear and dread at the prospect before him. He was utterly tired and found difficulty in thinking at all, let alone straight. The whole experience, the motion of the car, his fuddled brain and state of melancholy gave Andrew the feeling he was already asleep and in the centre of the worst nightmare of his life.

He opened his eyes, hoping to see his bedroom surrounding him with comfort but closed them again quickly again in order to try to forget the ghastly present. *It's at times like this that I believe in Heaven and Hell on Earth, and afterlife an escape from it all*, thought Andrew. He was finding that he envied Harry.

Chapter Twenty

As the police car reached the outskirts of Southwold, Andrew sat up and tried to pull himself together. He gazed out at the town lights as they turned the bend to go over Buss Creek towards the police station. He wished he could turn the clocks back and at that moment be lying securely in Susan's arms in her parents' house nearby, as he had been quite recently. Weariness overcame him again and with it a great, sad desire to blot out the present.

The detective in charge of the case grilled Andrew for hours on his relationship with Harry and their movements on the night he was drowned. They had already established the body was that of Harry from the evidence they found in his anorak, which still hung heavily on him when it washed up. A recent bill was folded in the top pocket and, though faint, could be read. The chandler from whom Harry had purchased items for the boat had checked the visa number on the bill and identified Harry's name. Having been told this, Andrew's hopes rose and he said with some relief,

'That means I don't have to identify the body, doesn't it?'

'I'm afraid you must. We have to be certain,' Andrew's heart fell to the pit of his stomach again,

'But surely it will be identifiable?' he began to plead, but was interrupted by the detective who stood up and took Andrew's elbow, showing little sympathy.

'Come on, you'd better do it now before you eat breakfast.'

He was sure he would not want to eat afterwards; his appetite for food had already deserted him anyway, hours earlier. In fear, trembling, and already feeling very sick despite his empty stomach he was led into the mortuary of the hospital near the police station. The police constable who had driven the few yards to it pulled back the sheet under which Harry's body lay. It took the little strength Andrew had left of his courage to glance at the corpse. Turning quickly away again and putting his face in his hands, he retched and sobbed at the same time. Andrew was led back to the waiting car and driven to the police station for further questioning. He still heaved each time the shrivelled vision of his friend came in unwelcome flashes into his mind.

'What were you doing out at sea at that time of night?' Inspector Ramsey asked, scrutinizing Andrew's face.

'Fishing. Night fishing.' Andrew told him.

'Yes, I know it wasn't day fishing at night,' the inspector said, sarcastically. The sergeant smiled. Andrew did not. He was becoming more nervous by the second.

'Come on, what were you up to?'

'I told you, fishing. You saw the bills for the tackle,' Andrew said, bluffing.

'Ah, but we didn't. I told you it was the bill from the chandler's, not the tackle shop.' *What are you angling for?* thought Andrew, despite his frenzied mind.

'Have you no more to say?' Inspector Ramsey asked Andrew.

'No, nothing more, except that I'd like something to eat now if I may. I'm starving!' he tried to smile.

'There's just one more thing I'd like you to see,' Ramsey said, getting out of his seat. He opened the cabinet next to him and pulled out a plastic packet. Andrew turned quite white and felt very faint. The Inspector observed his reaction with a wry smile.

'What then, do you know about this?' he asked, smirking.

'Nothing, what is it?' Andrew asked in a murmur, gripping his knees to stop himself shaking all over.

'I think you know what it is.' He emphasized, leaning over Andrew, almost snarling. Andrew backed away, gripping his thighs

'I don't know where it came from.'

'Perhaps not, but you know something about it, don't you? You'd better tell us all, the sooner we get this cleared up the better,'

'I'm supposed to be at work by now,' Andrew said, weakly.

'Don't worry about that. They know where you are. They won't be expecting you for some time,' Ramsey said, Andrew winced.

'Get him some food, and strong coffee, Brook, please.'

'Yes, Sir,' the sergeant said, making for the door. Andrew needed sustenance but would rather have died.

'I'm afraid we'll have to keep you in custody for the time being, until we get to the bottom of this,' Inspector Ramsey told a despairing Andrew. He was ushered into a small room and given a tray consisting of a large plate containing the usual breakfast fare, plus a mass of white bread and a huge mug of coffee. Andrew struggled to eat some of it, but, despite not having eaten for nearly 24 hours, he found difficulty in forcing it down. He felt so utterly miserable, turning the events of the past night and the night of the dreadful accident over and over in his mind. He wondered what Susan's reactions would be and those of her parents. He sobbed into his plate; disregarding the policeman he came to collect his tray of half eaten food.

The sergeant entered and, to Andrew's absolute horror, led him to a cell and locked him in, closing the door behind him before Andrew could object or rebel in any way. He felt in a daze, as if it was all happening to someone else and he was just playing the part for him.

'What the hell!' he yelled, when he cognized his position. 'Hey' he shouted, anger welling up within him, 'I need to phone my fiancé,' he explained to space, desperate for someone to hear him. A police constable opened the door and stood in its opening to prevent Andrew from flying through.

'What do you want?' he asked, unusually civil, Andrew thought.

'I must phone my fiancé,' he said again, almost in tears of desperation.

'No problem,' he assured Andrew, and went off to fetch it.

Andrew had to think quickly what he was going to say to Susan. He had to play the situation down. After all, the 'Law' as he called the police had no evidence against him. He began to feel more indignant as he summed up his situation. The constable came in with a mobile phone and stood there.

'OK, thanks,' Andrew said, hinting for the policeman to leave.

'We have to stay when our visitors are communicating to someone on the outside,' he explained. Andrew felt anger well up inside him again, but he was thwarted. He tentatively dialled Susan's number. She answered on the second ring, and, hearing his voice burst into tears, and in a hesitant, jittery voice, asked, 'Where are you? Why haven't you rung before? I've been at my wits end, ringing and ringing. No one from your office could or would tell me where you were. What's happened, Darling?' she went on at such a pace that Andrew could not interrupt her.

'It's all right, Darling; don't worry; only I couldn't ring before. I'm at the police station.' He told her, not wanting to tell her where. He did not want Susan's parents turning up and finding him in a police cell. That would be too humiliating for words. 'Where are you then?' Susan asked, sounding agitated. Andrew was forced to tell her.

'You poor thing,' Susan stressed 'poor' and started to cry again.

'How long will you be there, do you know? I'll come up tomorrow night for the weekend and you can rest at Ma's,' she told him.

'I don't know how long. It depends on when they finish questioning me. I might be here for days,' he said despondently. 'I'll try to ring you again tomorrow at your flat, so don't come up until I do,' Andrew told her, not wanting her to see him in a cell either.

'Good night, Darling, and don't worry. I am all right,' he continued, trying to convince himself as well as Susan.

'Good night, my Darling One. Don't forget I love you, and take courage,' she said, still crying.

'I love you too. Cheer up; I will be with you soon. Bye, Love.' Andrew said, resenting the policemen's presence while he was trying to comfort Susan. He put down the phone, murmured a depressed 'Thank you,' to the policeman as the latter removed the phone and himself.

Chapter Twenty-one

*A*ndrew lay on his bunk in his cell looking up at the ceiling and wished with all his heart that he had never agreed to Harry's suggestion of even buying the *Maggie*, let alone going out in it. He thought on this for some time with anger at his own folly. Tears trickled down the sides of his face into his hair. He wiped the wetness away with his hands and turned on his side. Utterly exhausted in body and mind he soon fell into a deep sleep. He was jolted awake two hours later, being shaken by a young constable. He felt a mixture of confusion, followed by fear, and deep depression. The last thing his body and soul wanted to do was get up, ever again. He forced his feet towards the floor.

'Come on Sir, hurry up. The inspector is back from lunch and he wants to see you, now.' He added, as Andrew took his time getting to his feet and rubbing his eyes. He was led into the small room for further interrogation. He had to think hard and as logically as possible despite being tired and despondent still. Again, he was questioned for hours, sometimes being asked the same thing repeatedly. The evidence, lying on the table between him and the Inspector, was devoid of fingerprints, which had long been obliterated by the salt water. Inspector Ramsey compelled

Andrew to re-live the trip out to sea and the last moments when they lost control of the *Maggie*, and Harry lost his life.

'I went to help him with the boat,' Andrew added, to try to give the impression he was being employed by Harry on that basis. He began to feel a little easier and more confident.

'Have you got the keys to your flat? I'm afraid we shall have to make a thorough search,' Ramsey said, scrutinising Andrew's face for a reaction, and holding out his hand. Andrew felt a fury well up inside him but tried to keep a calm exterior while feeling in his pocket for his keys.

'Am I being allowed to come with you?' he asked, wondering at the same time for how long he would be kept at the police station. He felt the situation would be easier at the weekend as far as Susan and her family were concerned if he was free. He started to detach his car keys from the ring while Ramsey stood with his hand out.

'Don't bother with that. We shall want to use those to go through your car as well. Where do you keep it? What colour is it? We've already got the registration number from Swansea.' He asked all these questions without answering Andrew's questions and before he could answer any of them.

'I keep it on the street outside the house. It's red.' He managed to tell the Inspector at last. He handed him the whole bunch of keys reluctantly, but in a nonchalant manner to try to show he had nothing to hide.

'When can I have them back?'

'I don't know. It depends on how things go. You'll have to stay in custody until we have checked all the evidence, and come to some decision.'

'Can't I be let out on bail?' Andrew asked naively.

'I'm afraid not. We shall probably have some more questioning to do during the weekend and even after that,' the Inspector told Andrew, showing little concern or sympathy. Andrew was returned to his cell to await further developments. He rang Susan on the mobile phone again and told her the situation. She could not understand why he was being kept there for so long.

'If they had made Harry's mother identify him they wouldn't have kept her in custody, so why you?'

'I'll explain when I see you, but don't come up this weekend, please Darling. Wait until I come down to you. I'll ring you as soon as I get home.' He wanted time to sort himself out, and to work out how he would play his cards when he did see her. At present, he could not think of a way to get out of the dreadful dilemma he was in.

Chapter Twenty-two

Susan felt very despondent and not at all in the mood for planning her wedding in less than two months' time. She was worried and confused. Time and time again, she wondered why Andrew was being kept at the police station. She could think of no reason why they should need him after he had identified the body.

After work, when back at her flat, Susan decided to ring her parents. She had hesitated the evening before, not wanting to worry them. When she had seen her mother off after their shopping spree she had told Jill she had too much to do to go home that weekend. Now she felt like flying into their arms for comfort. Andrew had told her to stay at her flat until he phoned to explain himself. She reflected on this, but, after much cogitation, she rang them.

'Hello my Girl, how are you?' her father asked.

'I'm all right Dad, thanks, but I'm worried about Andrew.' She explained to him the situation and he was startled to learn that Andrew was so near to them and had not rung them. They could have gone to see him and give him support, and indeed found out what the dilemma was.

'I'll ring the Chief, I know him quite well,' Bob told her.

'No, please don't do that Dad; wait until I get more news from Andrew. He is going to ring me as soon as he can during the weekend. Then I will know more. There might be quite a simple explanation. I will ring you back when he's rung and tell you what's happened. Is Mum there? I would like a word if possible. Bye Dad.'

'Bye my Dear, we'll await your call. You're not coming home then?'

'No, unless anything crops up and Andrew wants me up there.'

Susan waited while Bob called Jill, who was upstairs in her little sewing room. Her mother answered the phone in their bedroom.

'Hello, Darling. What news?' Susan explained all to her mother who immediately started to worry, as all mothers will.

'Shall I ask Dad to make enquiries for you? He knows some of the policemen here. He might go down and be permitted to speak to Andrew.'

'No, I've already asked Dad not to. Andrew will let me know what's happening and I'll ring you then.'

'Why don't you come up here, Darling, and be near him? I hate to think of you being up there all alone in that flat, or any other time for that matter,' Jill added.

'I'm all right Mum. I have loads to do here. Don't worry; I'll ring tomorrow when I get more news. Bye Mum, I love you both.' Susan rang off before her mother could say more. She sighed a deep breath of irritation. She wished she had not rung them after all. She always sensed when her mother was worried, even on the other end of the phone. Now she had caused her mother to worry unduly. *At least,* thought Susan, *I hope unduly*, then realised she was probably worrying unduly too, just like her mum, and smiled to herself. Jill ran downstairs in a mild state of panic, almost as if she enjoyed a little drama coming into their lives.

'Bob, what do you make of the situation? Do you think you ought to find out why they are keeping Andrew there all this time?'

'No need, until we hear more from Susan. It might be routine, though I cannot see what more they can find out after all this time. After all, they grilled Andrew enough when Harry drowned.'

Jill went to the kitchen to prepare the trout they were having for dinner. She became unusually quiet. Bob too, thought more than he spoke, but that was normal for him. He admitted to himself that he was puzzled by Andrew's detention at the police station. He laid the table as usual in the dining room and then sat down in the lounge waiting for the meal. A disturbing thought occurred to him. *What if the body had shown Harry did not drown, but was dead before the boat capsized? What if the evidence pointed to this?* He came back to the present when Jill called him into the dining room to come and eat.

They ate the meal, both deep in thought, hardly noticing the trout they were eating. Afterwards Jill packed the dishwasher and made coffee while Bob went back to his chair in the lounge. He picked up the book he was in the middle of reading when Jill came in with the coffee, so he would give the impression he was unconcerned. He, like his daughter, could easily sense when his wife was more than usually worried. He, too, felt uneasy. He opened the book at random, but the contents on page 48 were mere words in front of him. His eyes hardly focused on them, but his inner eyes were working overtime. Jill came in with the tray of coffee and placed it on the side table. She poured one out and handed it to Bob. As she was pouring her own she said suddenly, without glancing back,

'Darling, what if they have found new evidence and discovered that Harry died before the boat went down, and suspect Andrew of murder?' Bob was sipping his coffee and choked. The book fell down between his knees and he put his coffee cup down in haste on the small table by his chair. He pulled the handkerchief from his trouser pocket and blew his nose, trying to compose himself.

'Don't be silly, Darling. How could you think of such a thing?' he said, as if he hadn't.

'Well, we don't know him very well, do we? We haven't much knowledge of his background, only the little bit Susan told us. We have only known him since September. That's only six months,' she added, as if Bob was innumerate.

'We mustn't make conjectured, Love, it may be nothing,' Bob tried to change the conversation by asking Jill if she would like a Drambuie with her second cup of coffee. He knew it was her favourite liquor.

'I'd love one, thank you, Darling.' Bob got up and poured one, then bending over to hand her the tiny glass, he kissed her forehead, as he always did when in that position. He poured himself a brandy and went back to his seat. He picked up his book again and forced his mind to concentrate on the story, which eventually he succeeded in doing.

Jill took the tray to the kitchen and washed up the coffee things. She found she could not take her mind off Andrew and Susan and worried about her daughter and what she was letting herself in for by marrying him. She tried to look on the bright side and think of their last meeting and the medal he and Robert had won for bravery. She then went upstairs to continue for a while with her sewing. She was making her dress for the wedding, as she had found nothing in the shops she had liked. The materials were so drab, mostly of small or dreary flowers, like those her old mother used to wear, she thought. Instead, she'd bought some pale blue linen and a picture hat of fawn with fawn shoes to match. Thinking of these she soon cheered herself up and worked until very late, all the time concentrating on what she was doing to prevent her mind dwelling on her anxieties.

Bob deliberately tried to do the same, by continuing to read whilst listening to Brahms. From time to time he thought of what the future held for Susan and the worry for them all if Andrew was in some serious trouble. At last, he got up and went upstairs. He persuaded Jill to give up on her work for the day and go to bed. It had struck eleven on the old grandfather clock. They were both very tired and soon drifted away from the traumas of life.

Chapter Twenty-three

The police transferred Andrew back to the police station at Chigwell once local detectives working with Inspector Ramsey searched his flat and car. They found no evidence against him, which surprised them. To Harry's mother's distress, they went to her home and made a thorough search of his bedroom, attic and garage. From Harry's desk, they took away a briefcase of papers, and some files for examination. They also found the receipt given by Reggie for the sale of his boat; albeit on a piece of file paper written out by Harry and signed by Reggie in a scrawl which had indicated to Harry either his inability to put pen to paper or his reluctance to give his name to the transaction. Harry had failed to determine which.

Such as were the circumstances at the time when the receipt was found, that Reggie was located and taken to the police station in Southwold for questioning. He was justifiably het up and loudly stressed his innocence on everything relating to Harry's death other than he had sold him the old boat. Andrew had already informed the police that he had queried the safety of the craft, but that Harry had been confident it was seaworthy.

In fact, it was Harry who had been dubious in the first place but Andrew had lost the mate who could have argued against this accusation.

As the newspapers had hold of the story of Harry's body being washed up on the beach, the touring industry had become concerned that holiday makers would stay away. In fact, the opposite happened and they flocked there from Easter onwards, for weekends and longer periods. A morbid interest prevailed as with most events of this kind. The last thing Susan's parent's wanted was more publicity implicating Andrew. People in the town had been surmising many rumours already concerning the circumstances of the tragedy, most of these heard at second hand by Bob or Jill.

One or two acquaintances had even tactlessly asked them blatant questions which shocked Susan's parents, leaving them feeling quite miserable and hurt. They had no doubt whatsoever of Andrew's innocence and only at this time were they beginning to doubt their own judgement. A continuous uneasiness invaded their minds, especially when Susan rang them to say that Andrew had phoned her from the police station in Chigwell. She still had no inkling of the reason he was detained. He had evaded the questions from Susan with the excuse that he was not alone and could not talk freely. Even Susan was beginning to wonder what he had to hide from her and the police officer in his presence.

Susan was allowed to visit Andrew whilst he was at Chigwell and was very shocked at how tired and old he looked in so short a time. Still she learned nothing from him, being accompanied by a police sergeant for the duration of each visit. Her inquiries while there, to the Inspector, were as abortive. Each time she was told he was detained for questioning regarding the death of Harry. Each time she left feeling more and more frustrated and unhappy. The wedding was imminent and she felt she could make no further plans until she had more information on the outcome of Andrew's detention.

She went home the following weekend after Andrew's transfer to London, feeling completely washed out and deflated. They were all experiencing the strain of not knowing, feeling they were being kept in the dark.

'You look so tired, my Darling. Why don't you go up to bed early and get some rest?'

'Going to bed early doesn't help Mummy. I need to occupy myself, rather than lie there thinking. I do enough of that when I do get to bed later.'

'I wish to God we could get to the bottom of all this. I think I'll go down and have a word with someone I know. He might give some hint of why they are keeping Andrew so long. He's been there over a week now and we're no wiser. We can't be expected to go on like this,' Bob said. He walked up and down the room, staring at the carpet, with his hands stuffed deeply into his trouser pockets. This time Susan did not object. She desperately wanted some clarification of the situation.

'I can't think of why Andrew hasn't sent you a letter of explanation Darling. Surely he must know why he's being kept there. What has he got to hide?' Jill said miserably, and somewhat tactlessly.

'He said he couldn't write and tell me but would explain when he got a clear idea himself,' Susan said, feeling rather irritated by her mother's remark and feeling extremely frustrated.

'I'll go down in the morning, early. It's no good going as late as this. There'll be no one of any authority there at this time of night.'

While Jill cooked dinner, Bob took Susan for an evening walk. She expressed a wish to go out for a while and was glad when her father offered to come with her. They had always maintained a good rapport between them. Bob seemed to know and understand how his daughter felt without having to ask questions or catechize. Being a man of few words Susan felt safe and calmer, whereas her mother became het up and vented all her feelings and thoughts in a torrent. Bob knew that whatever advice or suggestion Susan wanted she would ask him without him having to prod her.

They walked through towards Buss Creek without passing the police station, then on towards Raydon. At the first pub they came to Bob invited his daughter to have a quiet drink with him there rather than walk further. He could see Susan was very weary and pensive and felt a whisky would cheer her up before they returned for dinner. During their wander back, Susan suddenly burst into tears and threw her arms around her father's neck.

'What shall I do Daddy, if we have to postpone the wedding? I've been so happy getting things ready.'

'Try not to worry about it at the moment, you have a month yet, time enough for things to be sorted out. I will do what I can in the morning to find out more. We must not get too pessimistic, dear Girl. I'm sure everything will sort itself out well soon.' He released his arms from around Susan and holding her shoulders, looked into her face. 'Dry your eyes, Love, don't let Mother see you've been crying or she will start.'

'Sorry Dad, it's not knowing that causes the tension to build up.'

'I know Love, I know.' Bob took her hand and wrapped his arm around hers. He patted the back of her hand and again smiled at her.

'Good old Dad,' Susan tried to smile and cheer herself up as they wandered homeward.

'You two have been gone a long time. How far did you go?' Jill asked, coming out of the kitchen wiping her hands on the towel.

'We had a drink in Raydon' Bob told her and kissed her.

'I'm dying to spend a penny,' Susan excused herself and ran upstairs so that she could rinse her face in cold water and wipe away any tell-tale signs that she had been crying. She took off her trousers, put on a skirt, and blouse for dinner.

'How was she?' Jill asked, as she dished up.

'She's OK, naturally a bit concerned, as we are.' Bob said.

'I rang Robert and told him what's going on,' Jill confessed.

'That was clever of you, considering we don't know ourselves. What did he say? How is he? When is he coming home?' Bob asked all of these questions without waiting for an answer to any of them.

'He seemed moderately surprised. He told us to keep him informed. He's fine, he was just in.'

'He's always just in when you ring him. You're too eager to get on the phone as soon as six o'clock arrives,' he smiled, pulling up his chair and pouring out the wine for all of them.

'Well, when I rang later, the other evening, he had just gone out again,' said Jill, trying to justify herself. Susan ran downstairs to join them, and, looking much more cheerful, sat down to eat.

Chapter Twenty-four

Next morning, Saturday, Bob rang up the police station and asked to speak to an officer he knew called George Carruthers. He was not there at that time but Bob was informed he would be in at eleven o'clock.

'Another wait,' Jill said, impatiently sighing. Bob went out to water the plants to keep himself occupied.

'Come and see how much I've done of my dress for the wedding, Darling,' Jill suggested to Susan to try to keep both their minds occupied. Susan thought this very tactless and almost snapped at her mother.

'No, thank you. I don't want to think of the wedding any more until I hear what information Daddy comes back with,' she said firmly. Both she and Jill were nervous, wondering what this would be. Jill dropped the subject of the wedding and instead concentrated on tidying the house, a task she wasted far too much time on, Bob often told her, to no avail.

Susan went upstairs, washed her hair, and spent the time combing it through and rubbing it dry with the towel. She looked in the mirror and was glad she did not have to go to a hairdresser to have it set. Then her mind turned again reluctantly to the wedding as she wondered how she would wear it on the day. When her hair was quite dry, she went downstairs.

They all drank coffee in the warm sun, sheltered from the cold breeze, on the patio where Susan's parents had first entertained Andrew. Susan sat stroking the side of her cup with her thumb and Jill was sitting with her right leg over the left one, rocking it back and forth like a pendulum. They were all obviously thinking back to that time in a pensive mood when the phone rang. Bob jumped up to answer it. As he had guessed, it was George Carruthers, who invited Bob across to see him straight away.

'That's very good of you, be with you in a few minutes.'

'Nice to see you Bob, sit down. How are things?' Carruthers asked, giving him a hearty handshake.

'A bit worrying at the moment, which is why I've come to see you,' Bob told him, sitting on the edge of the chair.

'Oh! How can I help?' he asked, frowning slightly and sensing an unusual tension in Bob's manner.

'I wonder if you could cast some light on the goings on of young Andrew Denby?' he asked bluntly. He observed the look of surprise in Carruthers, whose thick eyebrows shot up to meet his wrinkled forehead.

'How do you come to know him?' George interrupted before Bob had chance to tell him.

'My daughter is engaged to him. They are supposed to be getting married in just over a month's time,' Bob explained, leaning back on the chair to help him relax.

'Well, well! I see. Surprise, surprise, I had no idea.'

'Can you give me some idea of why he is being detained?' Bob came to the point, looking straight at Carruthers. George shifted in his seat uncomfortably.

'Well, I'm not really in a position to say, but if I give you a clue, you must keep it under your hat for the moment.'

'Of course, of course,' Bob began to feel hot and rubbed his left forefinger along under his collar. He sensed something unpleasant was about to be divulged to him.

'Well!' Carruthers began most of his sentences with 'well'. 'It's to do with the drowning of his friend Harry who has been recovered from the sea, as no doubt you have heard.' Bob felt he was evading the real issue. 'Yes, of course we all know that,' he said, hardly hiding his irritation. 'But what other evidence was found to warrant Andrew's detention for all this time?'

'Well, there's a question of drugs, I'm afraid.' Carruthers told him, somewhat embarrassed. 'But we still don't know whether or not Denby was involved at first hand.'

'Oh, my God!' Bob leaned forward in his chair and rested his forehead in his hands. For a long moment, he could not speak, but stared at the cord material of his trousers, his whole mind seemed to him to be suddenly swept into another dimension, as if it had entered Hell and in the middle of a tangle of fibre, from which he could not escape. His body lost its composure and he fought hard not to cry out or indeed to cry. He heard Carruthers speak, and his nightmare state was partly broken.

'I'm sorry this has come as a great shock, Bob. I can understand your feelings, but you must remember that we are still trying to gather evidence and nothing has yet been solved.' George came round his desk and squeezed Bob's shoulder.

'You must have some idea that Andrew was implicated to have kept him this long,' Bob reasoned, in despair.

'Well yes, I admit that, of course. You see, we found some cannabis on the body.'

'This is too awful. How am I going to break the news to my daughter? I just don't know, or my poor wife,' Bob added, feeling in complete despair at the thought of doing so. He rubbed his face with his hands and sat up straight looking very white.

'Would you like me to have a word with her for you? Or do you think it's better not to tell her at the moment until we get some positive results from our enquiries?' he suggested, trying to think of an immediate solution to help Bob.

'They're both waiting for me to return with some information. I won't be able to hide my distress. Poor kid, I can't think how she will take it, but I shall have to face that when I tell her. I must at least warn her even if I can play it down a bit. I can't see how the Boy can fail to be implicated, little bugger,' Bob emphasized with feeling. He got up out of his chair with the lethargy of someone having been knocked about in the boxing ring.

'I'm surprised Denby didn't let on that his fiancée came from here. He spoke to her in London once or twice, I remember. I was surprised when you told me who she was,' Carruthers said, following Bob to the door.

'I don't suppose he's very proud of himself at the moment. He wouldn't want us to know the truth.' Bob turned round to shake hands with Carruthers and forced a smile.

'Thanks for this, Old Boy. I'll go and have a swift drink before I go home.'

'Bye Bob. If I can help in any way give me a ring,' George said, feeling somewhat helpless.

'Thanks. Perhaps you'll call me when you get some positive information. Susan will have to decide what to do about the wedding soon. There's not much time.' Bob told him miserably.

'All the best Bob,' George said with sincerity as Bob left the building. Very reluctant to get home to impart the dreadful news of Andrew's actions Bob made his way with heavy heart and feet to the Southwold Arms, which he seldom frequented, and so no one would recognize him. He needed to be left alone to think, though he was in such depressed turmoil that he found this difficult. He drank a double whisky as he was without his car, and tried to visualise Jill's and Susan's reaction when he told them of the terrible news. As he walked home in a dream, weighed down by his heavy heart, he tried to pull himself into some sort of deceiving presence, hoping to make his response to his questions at the police station less devastating for Jill and Susan. They were sitting on the patio where he had left them, and they were drinking sherry.

'Have you two been sitting here since I left?' he asked them, smiling, and trying to calm his turbulent insides.

'Did you get the information?' Jill asked, without answering his question.

'It's bad news, isn't it? She asked, easily reading his face.

'Not good as far as they can ascertain at present,' Bob said, staring at the patio slabs as he pulled his chair under him.

'For goodness sake, tell us. Don't keep us in this awful suspense. You know you can't hide much from Susan and the sooner we know the better.'

'Drugs, I'm afraid. Drugs.' Bob heard himself saying without emotion.

'What are you saying, Daddy? That Andrew was involved in drugs?' Susan asked, in complete disbelief. He nodded.

'At least, nothing is proven yet, but it looks like that, Susan.' He told her, glancing in her direction but not able to look her full in the face. She put her face in her hands as her father had done and began to sob.

'I can't believe it. It can't be true. Why would he? There must be some mistake,' she cried through her handkerchief. Jill got up and put her arm around Susan's shoulder while Bob just sat like a worn out teddy bear. He became unable to communicate further and left that to Jill.

'We must find out more as soon as possible. We cannot go on in this limbo. They can't expect us to.' She moaned.

'They'll ring us.' Was all Bob could bring himself to say.

'I'll make a salad for lunch,' Jill said needlessly.

They ate very little.

Chapter Twenty-five

Susan stayed at her parents' house for most of the following week. They had persuaded her not to return to work or her flat and be alone with her troubles. She could not believe that Andrew was in any way implicated in drug smuggling, and waited impatiently for the police to confirm this to her. Jill, although very distressed, was a little relieved it was not murder, which at one point had entered her mind, and she guessed Bob's too. Mulling this over between them later when they had all retired to bed they realised drug trafficking was much worse.

'They kill more than one, and young people at that, indirectly, but knowingly,' Bob whispered.

'And devastate the youngsters' families and often their own too, and all for greed,' Jill sad miserably, and burst into tears again. Bob slid his arm under his wife and she sobbed onto his chest. He lay there thinking of poor Susan who was alone in her room along the corridor with no one to comfort her. They fell asleep eventually, worn out by their sorrows. Susan lay awake thinking of how despicable are the unscrupulous and selfish scum of the earth who can blatantly exploit sad, vulnerable people, causing them in their desperation to steal to get big money to pay for their own destruction. Her mind went on in this vein without pause, wondering what possible joy the exploiters could gain at the end of it all.

Andrew came back into her depressed mind. If he was involved, she could not reason why. He told her he had a good job. He never seemed to need money. She could not believe he would get involved for pure greed, putting himself down to the level of the rest. *There must be some big mistake,* she thought with a fraction of hope entering her distraught body. She then turned her mind to their wedding and burst into tears again until she fell asleep on a very wet pillow, in utter exhaustion. These thoughts invaded all their minds day and night until the Thursday when George Carruthers telephoned Bob to ask him to meet him at his office at 10.30.

'May I come with you, Daddy? I'd like to,' Susan asked, not wanting to stay at home waiting in trepidation for his return.

'I'd wait here, Love, if I were you. Stay with your mother, please. I think you would be better here until I get back. I won't be long.'

'OK, we'll go for little walk perhaps,' Susan agreed reluctantly. Her mother came downstairs and joined them while Bob was getting his coat on to leave.

'Go for a short walk with Susan until I get back. It'll be easier than hanging around here waiting,' he said.

'Yes, Darling, I do hope the news will be good,' she commented, unnecessarily.

Bob went off wondering what news he would be returning with, while Jill and Susan got their coats on, locking the door behind them, and set off and took one of the many footpaths along and around Buss Creek where they could almost certainly guarantee to be alone at that time of day. When Bob arrived back he found them still out and looking at his watch realised he had been away for only forty minutes. He went to the kitchen and put the kettle on for some coffee, the hour being too early for stronger fortification. Susan and Jill returned home when he had boiled the kettle and prepared the craftier. He carried the tray to the lounge and poured out the coffee without saying anything. Then he walked towards Susan, held her shoulders and was about to speak when she interrupted him, staring into his face.

'It's true, I can see by your face, Daddy.' She fell into his arms. He held her closely with one arm and put the other around his wife, who was also breaking down. He held them both like this for some moments. Susan broke away from them and ran up to her room. She threw herself onto her bed and sobbed uncontrollably. Jill and Bob went to the sofa and sat down. Bob put his arms around her to try and comfort her but had little comfort in his own soul to give. They left Susan to cry her utter misery out of her body as far as it was possible. She ultimately fell into a deep sleep, quite exhausted from sobbing and from nights of disturbed sleep. They did not wake her for lunch and could eat very little themselves. Later, when they were all together again and composed enough to talk, they drank tea in the lounge while Bob painfully explained to them what information he had gleaned from George Carruthers.

'Apparently, Andrew was influenced by Harry whom he had heard at work boasting about his material possessions. The fatal trip was definitely the first one for Andrew. Some old boy in the area vouched for that. He sold them the old boat and had sometimes watched them doing her up.' Here Jill interrupted,

'You see, Darling, it was them we saw on the far Walberswick bank when we went out for the walk that time. Do you remember? I mentioned it then.'

'When did you see them? Why didn't you tell me?' Susan peered from one to the other through red, tear-stained eyes.

'We weren't sure. It was late evening and the light was too bad to tell for certain,' Bob explained. He went on; 'apparently Harry had been involved in this business for some time.' Bob avoided having to say the word 'drugs'. 'He was working with another group elsewhere along the coast and wanted his own boat. He was only too glad to have Andrew join him.'

'But how could he? That is what I do not understand. Where were his scruples?' Jill asked. Susan and Bob did not comment on this pointless question, for which they obviously had no answer.

'What's going to happen to Andrew then?' Susan asked with great pain in her heart.

'They don't know yet. Obviously they'll have to take him to court as an accomplice at least.' Bob told her. He forced himself to tell her the truth of the matter so that she could come to terms with her own situation as soon as possible.

'That means we can't get married now,' Susan said, in a flat, defeated tone, her bottom lip quivering. Jill hoped she wouldn't want to anyway in the circumstances, but bit her tongue from saying so.

'I'm afraid not, dear Girl. You'll have to postpone it until the whole affair is cleared up.' Bob tried to be tactful but was thinking along the same lines as Jill.

'If he's found to be guilty I won't marry him anyway,' Susan said, to their great relief. In the realisation of what this will mean, Susan broke down completely in front of her parents. They tried to pacify her as best they could but in such a terrible, traumatic time such as this, there is little one can do but let time take its toll.

'I'll get you a whisky, Love,' Bob said, feeling useless.

'I'll have a big gin and tonic, Darling, please.'

'I didn't have to ask you, I know,' he smiled sadly at his wife. He poured himself a whisky as well and they sat miserably together, not saying very much but all thinking of the situation Susan was in and wondering what the final outcome would be. She did not wish to contact Andrew and indeed felt very angry that he should let her down with such a cruel bump without giving her any warning when they had talked together at the police station and on the phone during the past agonizing two weeks. She felt embittered by his unscrupulous action in getting involved with a drug trafficker, and of deceiving her. No doubt, this would help her overcome her loss of someone she dearly loved in the long run but at that moment, the hurt he had caused was unbearable. She could not eat her lunch and went upstairs to lie on her bed again in dreadful, unhappy despair.

Bob and Jill felt a mixture of desperate sadness for Susan, great anger at Andrew for causing such devastation to them all, yet some relief at Susan's determination to end the relationship. At least that was her plan at present and they hoped that later, when the trauma and unhappiness caused to her diminished slightly, that she would not change her mind.

'After all, she does love him, and love plays a large part in a relationship in both partners,' Bob reasoned.

'I should think she will hate him for evermore. There is a limit to how much a person can tolerate. She will never be able to trust him to be straight and honest with her. Without that, life is best lived on one's own. It's better to be content than waste life trapped with someone in unhappiness.' Bob took her hand and pressed it to his lips.

'Yes, we are lucky my love. I just hope both our children will eventually find the degree of happiness we've found together.'

Chapter Twenty-six

Andrew sat on his bunk in his cell with his elbows on his knees, running his hands through his hair. He wished with all his heart he had never agreed to Harry's suggestion of trying to make quick money. His one aim had been to give Susan a better standard of living than he would be able to give on his salary. He dreamed of a big flat, in a nice environment in London, in giving her the style of living in which she had been brought up. He had even thought of buying her a small yacht as a wedding present. Such big ideas had led him to this. His mind and body felt wretched. He continually thought back on the circumstances leading up to the ruination of his life, which he now wanted to end. Sometimes he still felt like he was living in a dream, a dreadful dream.

When Andrew had hinted to his friend that he seemed affluent than he on the same salary, Harry at first told him that he had inherited a large sum. In fact, that was the story that Andrew heard round the office when Harry turned up in an expensive sports car to work.

It was later, when Andrew had mentioned to Harry that his girlfriend came from an affluent middle class family that Harry had offered to help him by confessing his source of income. At first Andrew had been appalled, but then, having thought about the idea of gaining quick money he had approached Harry and Harry had bought Reggie's boat for that purpose. Andrew had not intended to carry on this despicable venture for very long as Harry had done, but only to get a sum in hand before his marriage to Susan. He now realised his morals had deserted him in his endeavour to make Susan happy. Ironically, in the circumstances, he will have caused just the reverse. He stood up and walked up and down the small area that was his living space, for how long he could not and would not guess. After picking over his lunch and eating very little of it, Andrew was again taken into the small room for questioning. He had to think hard and as logically as possible despite being tired and completely despondent. Again, he was asked from whom the cannabis came, and again he truthfully said he did not know, except that Harry told him that it came from Holland.

Harry had deliberately refused to tell Andrew the source of the drugs and Andrew did not wish to know or to be implicated to that extent. He only wished that Harry had not pocketed one of the packets of the stuff and asked himself why Harry would have done so. Perhaps he had grabbed it at the last minute when the boat was breaking up, but he did not know how many moments Harry had had before he was swept into the depths of the sea.

'Did you get some of the drugs too?' Andrew was asked.

'No, none,' he answered truthfully.

'Were you hoping to?'

'I was hoping to get a cut from the sale of it indirectly,' he confessed, without admitting he was an accomplice.

'What do you mean, 'indirectly'?'

'Well, I told you before, I went with him to help on the boat and he was going to pay me,' Andrew was again trying to give the impression he was employed by Harry. He was getting irritated by being asked the same questions.

'When am I going to be out on bail?' Andrew asked, hoping to go to Susan and ask for her forgiveness. 'Perhaps when she realises my motives she will understand,' he was thinking to himself.

'Who the hell do you think will stand your bail, your fiancée?' the inspector shouted, snarling across the table at Andrew, 'We have little sympathy with drug pushers,' Andrew could sense this without being told. His heart sank into the soles of his shoes.

'They're despicable. Making money on other people's weakness. Even causing them to die,' Ramsey shouted even louder, to push his feelings on the subject deeper into Andrew's brain.

'I know. I wish I'd never got involved with Harry,' Andrew said weakly, but with feeling. He sighed with fatigue and bent his head, staring into his lap with despair.

'Get up and go back to your cell. Take him away, Sergeant.' The inspector ordered in a despising tone of anger. Andrew realised now what it was like to be a real criminal, to be locked away from society and living in one small room with nothing to commend it. This ghastly realisation hit him very hard, like a cricket ball landing in the middle of his stomach. He held his middle with both hands as if the simile was real and followed the sergeant back to his cell, shuffling his feet, and with head bent in both shame and despair.

For days, Andrew could eat very little and only spoke when necessary. Then he was moved to Pentonville Prison and put into a cell with two other men. He was even more disinclined to speak despite the two prisoners trying to ask him questions and get him involved in their limited conversation topics. He spent the days thinking of Susan and not daring to ring her, and hoping she would not find out where he was. On the other hand, he was somewhat perturbed that she would have worried where he had gone without ringing her to say. He had no idea that she knew of his crime. Part of his mind wanted to phone her and confess all to her. He desperately longed to hear her voice. He knew it would be a happy sound, as he had always loved to hear it when she spoke to him.

When he had become a little more accustomed to his surroundings and the forced closeness of Dan and Bill, who shared his cell, Andrew slowly opened up and began joining in on their chats. It was then that he felt more inclined to write a letter to Susan and tell her all, at the same time dreading her response for fear of the almost inevitable rejection of him.

Susan received Andrew's letter in a state of trepidation. Having picked it out of her postbox in the main hall of the flats in which she lived, she put each foot heavily on the stairs, reluctant to reach her door. She pushed it open and banging it shut with her elbow she went to the kitchen, laid the envelope on the table and put the kettle on. She picked up the envelope again. Her hands were shaking. Tears welled up when she saw the printed words, 'H.M.P. Pentonville' blurred through wet lashes. She tore it open. Still she hadn't the courage to take the letter out of the yellow envelope. When the kettle boiled, she made herself some coffee. Again picking up the letter, she made her way to the lounge and sat down in the armchair.

After taking a few sips of coffee, Susan tentatively took the letter from the envelope and slowly opened it out. She read it slowly, as if she found difficulty in reading at all. It contained exactly all that she imagined it would, and the fact that what he had done was meant for her benefit. This made her very angry. The resentment welled up within her. Tears also welled up and dropped onto the page as if wanting to wash away the words and all they implied. Susan dropped her hands into her lap still holding the letter. She threw it on the floor and curled up in her chair, resting her head on the left arm of it and sobbed bitter tears of hopelessness and utter dejection. She jumped when the phone rang beside her. She let it ring for a few seconds wondering whether to answer it or not. She hesitantly picked it up and said, 'Hello?' in a flat voice.

'Hi Sue, it's me,' she recognised Robert's voice.

'Where are you?'

'In Aldershot. I thought I'd have a word. Ma told me of Andrew's goings on. I'm sorry Sis', to hear about it. Sue?, Are you still there?'

'Yes, Robert.' She could not stop crying. 'Oh, Rob, what am I going to do? I wish you were here.'

'Don't cry, Love. I am coming home next week. I thought as the wedding was off I'd get leave a bit earlier so I can be with you for a few days. Cheer up, Old Thing,' Gladness entered Susan's heart and she managed to say, between sudden convulsive inhalations of breath caused by crying so much,

'I'm so glad, Rob, that's super of you. I need you so much at this time. My whole life has come apart in the last two weeks.'

'What on earth was he thinking about? Do you think he's been doing this for long? Did you have any inkling or hindsight? Can you remember anything that would throw any light on what he was doing?

'He says in the letter I've just received that he did it to give me a good living standard after we were married. I feel furious about this, as if he were putting the blame on me. I told him I wasn't interested in material things, Rob. He did say, I remember, that he would get a big flat for us, in a nice area, but he always gave the impression that he was well off financially anyway.'

'I wonder if it was true, what Pop was told, that it was Andrew's first time out. Do you know Sue, I'll tell you now, my friend John and I saw him going out once in an old fishing boat,'

'What?!' Susan interrupted her brother in disbelief, 'Why didn't you tell me that at the time? That must have been before Christmas time when you were home?'

'Yes, that right. To tell you the truth, I questioned him on the fact that I had seen him, at our house, a short time after, and he told me he was on a secret mission from work, going out to investigate smuggling going on, seen by some fishermen. When I said that I thought that was the coastguard's job, he said he was in liaison with them, and they used the fishing boat as a disguise. He told me not to say anything to anyone. I wonder if he was smuggling himself at that time.'

'Good heavens, Robert, did you tell Mummy and Daddy? Why didn't you tell me?'

'Honey, because it would have been difficult for you not to mention it at some point, however well-intentioned initially. I only told our parents it was a secret and nothing to worry about.' Susan blew her nose and felt too angry and confused to cry anymore.

'I'm glad you told me now. In the circumstances I'll write him a note and tell him the engagement is off and I want nothing more to do with him.' She felt quite resolute on this.

'It's what he deserves, but wait a while Sis', until you can see everything in a more rational light, more objectively.'

'No way am I going to marry him now. I could never trust him again. He has deceived me more than once I am sure. He's often told me he was working late and couldn't come over to see me. At times, I wondered if he had another woman. I bet he was either drug trafficking then, or planning it. Yuk.'

'What on earth was that noise for, Sue?'

She smiled, 'I sipped my coffee and it was stone cold,' she explained, and added, 'it will do to show how I feel about bloody Andrew too. You must go Rob; you've been on the phone for ages.'

'It's OK, Susie, I don't mind, you're worth it.'

'Thanks Robert. I do appreciate it. You've cheered me up and given me information that makes me even more determined not to see Andrew again. And to think I felt sorry for him working so hard! My God Robert, I'll be glad when you are here. Which day are you coming?'

'I don't know yet, I'll ring you, probably Friday.'

'Good, I will come to Liverpool Street to pick you up if you let me know the time of arrival. I can't wait to see you. I'm glad there are at least two men I can go on loving, who are decent. Bye Rob.'

'Bye Sis', I love you, too. Chin up, and I'll see you next week.'

Susan put the phone down and went to the kitchen to make herself some fresh coffee, tears streaming down her face.

Chapter Twenty-seven

*A*ndrew too felt very uneasy as he fumbled with the envelope he had received from Susan. Recognising her handwriting, he sat on his bunk staring at the address she had painfully written on it. *God, if only this were a dream and I was at home*, he thought miserably. *If only she'll forgive me and we can forget the whole bloody business and be happy again.* He thought about his immediate future, of the court case and the outcome. He knew that, even if Susan still wanted to marry him, the wedding would have to be put off until he came out of prison, whenever that would be.

'You're not very keen to open your letter Andrew,' Bill had been watching him staring into space, with a woebegone look on his face.

'I'll open it later,' he murmured, slipping the envelope under his pillow. Dan was re-reading his mail, also absorbed in thought. 'Bugger, bugger, bugger!' he exclaimed suddenly. He screwed up the letter, buried his head in his pillow, and started to sob.

'What's up, Mate?' Bill asked, going over to Dan's bed and touching his shoulder. For a while, he continued to sob, his body heaving. Andrew looked on non-committally, wondering what his own reaction would be when he had read Susan's letter.

'What's up?' Bill asked again, feeling helpless.

'My Old Girl's leaving me and going off with the kids,' Dan managed to blubber. He sniffed and blew his nose, then lay in a helpless, dejected heap on the bed.

'I'm sorry Mate,' was all Bill could say, and returned to his bunk. Andrew glanced at them both in turn but could say nothing.

'What a bloody miserable start to the day,' Bill said at last.

'Worse than usual,' Andrew commented.

'You'd better open yours up now Andy; we might as well all be in hell at the same time, Mate,' Bill said solemnly.

'I'll wait until later,' was all Andrew said.

'I'm bloody glad I didn't have a steady bird before I came in here. Bad enough losing them in normal circumstances,' Bill said.

'You're sodding lucky you two haven't got kids either,' Dan blubbered.

Bill felt a little uneasy, remembering he had a son somewhere but unable to accept the responsibility for him and the young mother, had made himself scarce and left her to bear the brunt. He wondered how different his life might have been if he had faced up to his duty to the girl and their child. He might have been happily married now, and not succumbed to evil influences which had landed him where he was, sitting with other wrongdoers all of every day.

The motley inmates, with no regard for others' mental or physical turmoil and themselves devoid of shame, performed the prison duties. The prison officers made comments to them, if, like Dan, any of them seemed more than usually morbid. They were taken to the workshops and given tasks to occupy them for much of the day. Andrew had left his letter, still unopened, under his pillow to be read when he could summon the courage to do so. Dan had been told the work would take his mind off his trouble but he did not find it so and spoke to no one all day, but enveloped his thoughts and misery within himself. He did little but wander around or sit on one of the stools with his head down. The officers would not allow him to retreat to his cell alone but eventually left him to drown in his resentment. He ate nothing all day and back in their cell in the early evening, Dan slid inside his bed without even undressing properly.

From time to time Bill and Andrew could hear Dan sobbing pitiably under his bedclothes and felt utterly miserable for him and themselves. When he and Bill had at last fallen asleep Andrew felt under his pillow for Susan's letter, but still could not find the courage to open it. He lay awake for a long time trying to think of what his reaction would be if she forsook him and what he would do. At last, he crept out of bed unable to wait longer to know the contents of the letter. He went to the barred window for more light to enable him to read it. Slowly he opened the envelope, not wanting to awaken his cellmates. He unfolded the letter and saw it was short in content. Forcing his eyes away from scanning the page as a whole to get the gist of what was written there, he read slowly;

Andrew,

I am utterly disgusted by what you have done. Even more so that you tell me you did this despicable thing for my benefit. How could you transfer some of your blame onto me? That in itself is despicable. I resent being a scapegoat for your actions. You have caused unforgivable unhappiness to me, and to also my family. We are all devastated, especially so near to the wedding date.

You deceived me and lied to my brother at a time when I was happily preparing for our wedding. The only good thing that has come out of all this is that I found out about your true character before becoming your wife.

No doubt by now you realise that the wedding is off, permanently. It is a great pity you acted without thought for all those sad souls whose lives you would have ruined through drugs, as well as having ruined my life and no doubt your own. Do not contact me ever again. I want to try to forget I loved you.

Susan

Andrew screwed up the letter, just as Dan had done with the one from his wife that morning. He did not break down and cry. His mind felt too numb for that. He glanced across at his two cellmates who were sound asleep. Back on his bed, Andrew sat with his head in his hands, as he had often done since being in prison. Eventually, he quietly got into bed and lay on his back staring at the ceiling, until his eyes closed and he fell asleep, free of the ghastly thoughts that had perpetuated in his mind since his confinement in the self-made hell in which he now existed. He woke with a splitting headache to the din of the officers calling them up. He crawled out of bed mumbling a greeting to Dan and Bill and made his way to the loo attached to the cell which the three of them used.

'Have you not read your letter yet?' Bill inquired when Andrew reappeared.

'Yes. She's finished with me,' Andrew told him, sombrely.

'Join the effing club,' Dan said loudly, as he crawled out of bed reluctantly, looking bedraggled in the day clothes he had gone to bed in.

'Those bloody garments look bad enough in the daytime, without making them look worse by sleeping in the buggers,' Bill said coarsely.

'They're good enough for this hell hole. I haven't seen you wear your best suit on Sundays,' Dan retorted. Andrew was excused from workshop duties. His head was worse and he could eat no breakfast.

'They didn't excuse me yesterday when I felt like bloody hell,' Dan moaned as Andrew was led back to his cell. 'One rule for the likes of us and one for the so-called white-collar bastards like him who murder with drugs, not guns,' he added resentfully.

'Enough of that! Get going.' The officer ordered him.

Andrew was locked in his cell and left to recover.

Chapter Twenty-eight

Susan's manager advised her to take the next two weeks off to be with her family, in lieu of the time she was to have taken for her wedding and honeymoon the following month. She found she could not concentrate at work, nor could she feel anything but utter dejection, which caused her workmates to feel depressed and sorry for her.

She accepted the offer and packed a few clothes, diverting her eyes from the new items she had so happily acquired for her new life with Andrew. Glad to get out of her flat and all that reminded her of her collapsed relationship she locked the door and ran down the stairs, out of the block and to her car. On route to her parents, Susan wondered, for the umpteenth time since she had written it, what Andrew's reaction would be when he read the letter. She then turned her mind to her arrival home to tell Bob and Jill what she had written to him, and her thoughts then turned to Robert's homecoming in a few days and her heart became less heavy. She wished he was going to be there when she got home so that her parent's attention would not be entirely upon her, and they too would find some happiness in having him with them. As it was, and as Susan had expected, Bob and Jill came to the car to greet her with forced smiles breaking their sad faces.

'Good to have you with us, Darling,' Jill said, hugging Susan for some moments. She then fell into her father's arms and the tears could no longer be held back. Jill began to cry when she saw Susan's tears and Bob took their arms gently and led them into the house. He handed them paper handkerchiefs and poured them all a stiff drink. They all sat together on the settee, with Susan in the middle. Bob put his arm around her and Jill held her hand. The settee was rocking with Susan's sobs as she unwound the heartache she had until now partly controlled by the feelings of anger Andrew had caused to fester within her.

'The two good things that have come out of this is that you found out about his character in time and that he has been thwarted in his selfish attempt to cause suffering to other people,' They told her.

'They'll get it from some other source,' Susan whispered, wiping her eyes.

'The suppliers should be decapitated. I believe they are in South America or Asia,' Jill said tactlessly. Bob frowned at her over Susan's head, but she tried to smile through her tears.

'I don't think I would wish to hear Andrew had had his head chopped off, despite everything,' she was half crying and half laughing at her mother's comment.

'Of course not. Sorry, Darling,' Jill said, but went on, 'since drug taking has become so wide spread the users will do anything to get the money for it, that's why there is so much robbery and violence nowadays.' Her comments were so platitudinous, the world being as aware of this as she was, that Bob got up in order to change the conversation and to refill their glasses. Handing Jill her drink, he asked,

'Is lunch nearly ready, Love, I'm pretty hungry.' Jill let go of Susan's hand and stood, smiling down at her,

'Yes, it's salad so I will only have to take it into the dining room. It's all ready.'

She put down her glass and went upstairs to powder her nose and Susan followed to wash her face in her bedroom basin. She waited until she heard her mother go downstairs before she emerged. She did not want to be alone in her mother's company at that moment in case she said anything to start them both off crying again. They ate lunch saying very little. Occasionally Jill reached across and stroked Susan's back in a supportive gesture, and Bob squeezed her hand when Jill went to the kitchen to fetch dessert.

'At what time is Robert arriving Friday, Dad?' Susan fingered her glass stem.

'Not until six in the evening, I don't think.'

'I'd like to go down and meet him at Victoria,' Susan told him.

'You can come down with us of course, Darling,' Jill said smiling as she arrived with the fruit salad and cream.

'I'd really like to go on my own, so we can be alone and get our talking about Andrew over on the way, before we get home,' Susan said tentatively. 'If you don't mind, that is,' she added, noticing the look of disappointment on Jill's face. 'You've had enough of seeing me upset and I'm bound to be so again when I see Rob,' She told them, hoping that would soften the blow for her mother.

'Of course, my Girl. He is coming home for your sake. We'll wait here for you both, won't we, Darling?'

'Yes, all right,' Susan detected a note of reluctance in her mother's voice but said nothing. After lunch, Susan went up to her room to unpack. She then flopped onto her bed and, quite exhausted from the traumas of her present life, fell into a deep sleep. Jill woke her up with a cup of tea at five o'clock.

'I left you asleep as long as possible but I thought you wouldn't sleep tonight if I left you any longer, Darling.'

'I could sleep a thousand years,' Susan smiled, trying to hide her irritation at being brought back to consciousness and her unhappy state.

'There's some cake downstairs. We have started tea but you take your time. There's no hurry,' Jill told her. Susan knew they liked tea about 4 o'clock as they usually ate dinner early, at about seven. Then they could go to the television room when there was anything they wanted to watch.

When that time came, Susan accompanied them in order to try to forget her troubles. She felt unsettled, however, which her parents sensed. Her mind frequently floated back to Andrew, setting her mind in turmoil. At one moment she felt angry and at another on the verge of tears at the thought that her life had fallen to shreds. In fleeting moments she felt glad that she was away from him and in the security of her own home and family. Robert would be home at the weekend and that thought alleviated some of the physical pain her situation had created within her. She longed for him to be there. She longed for his brotherly support.

Susan slept fitfully that night and arose late. Apparently, Bob and Jill were also late as they were still at the breakfast table when she made an appearance there. Jill poured her some coffee and Susan ate a little muesli, then helped herself to an egg, and grilled tomatoes from the hotplate on the sideboard. Jill was pleased to see her eating well.

The letterbox clattered and Susan got up to get the mail. Instead, she picked up the newspaper from the mat.

'It's late today, for some reason,' Bob said as he saw *The Telegraph* in Susan's hands. She glanced down the page as she entered the room then took it to hand to her father who always read it first at the breakfast table. She stared at the bottom of the page, gave a weak cry, and slid down the door surround to the floor in a dead faint. Jill and Bob jumped up from their chairs and ran to help her.

'She's passed out,' Jill squeaked, 'quick, get her onto the settee,' Bob picked Susan up in both arms and laid her on the settee with a cushion under her head. Jill rushed in with a glass of water and the box of paper hankies. The newspaper lay crumpled on the floor where she had dropped it and Bob had trodden on it. Susan came to and looked, bewildered, from one to the other.

'Oh no, Mummy!' was all she said before passing out again.

Jill brought her round with the smelling salts she had grabbed from the kitchen medicine cabinet, and mopped her brow. Bob snatched up the newspaper and scanned the front page.

'My God,' was all he could mutter as he stared at the headline, 'Man found hanged in prison cell.'

Jill and Bob tried to pacify Susan, but could find nothing positive to say. She gave her a warm cup of tea but Susan could not be persuaded to eat her breakfast, she lay on the settee with her face buried in a cushion, and was inconsolable. Jill quietly wept into the hanging towel in the kitchen so that Susan should not hear her, and Bob paced up and down, lost in his inability to be of much comfort. Indeed, he too, needed comforting, a privilege men seldom get, unless they are the immediate victims.

Bob then decided to take some action if only to telephone the police. He walked heavily upstairs to use the phone in his bedroom so that Susan could not hear his conversation and rang the officer at Southwold Station hoping to gain some first-hand information of the ghastly death of Susan's ex- fiancé. He learned that one of the prison officers had discovered the body on a routine check of the cells after Andrew had complained of a bad headache and been excused workshop duties.

'They found a letter to your daughter on the bed but as you had expressed the wish for no correspondence from him to her, the Governor is sending it on in an envelope addressed to you.'

'Good, thanks, George. I will have to read it and use my discretion whether to show it to Susan or not. Has he sent it off yet?'

'I'm not sure, but I should think you'll get it tomorrow, I'm so sorry about all this, Bob. Give my sincere sympathy to your daughter, in fact from all of us here.'

'Thanks, she's taking it very badly. I am jolly grateful all of this has come out before the wedding. It would have been much worse if she had already married him.' Bob wanted to say 'the swine' but refrained. He realised the terrible state Andrew's mind must have been in, the guilt, and utter futility in going on living that he must have felt. 'Bye George, thanks again.' Bob said in a dull voice and slowly put down the phone. Bob slept that night in Susan's room while Susan stayed with her mother, so that Jill could comfort her. None of them slept very much. At three o'clock Bob heard Jill and Susan talking so got up and made them all a cup of tea. Feeling utterly saddened they got up at dawn, tired of their beds. They looked as if their faces had dropped onto their lower jaws, so miserable and exhausted did they look.

Susan would still eat nothing but Jill and Bob ate cereal and toast, having had, like Susan, very little appetite the day before. When the postal man arrived, Bob went to the hall to pick up the mail and scanning quickly through it came to the envelope marked Pentonville Prison. He slipped it into his trouser pocket so that neither Susan nor Jill would see it. He would read it later when he was alone in his study.

Jill wanted to call the doctor in to see Susan and give her a sedative so that she could get some sleep and rest her tortured mind but she would not hear of it. She knew she would fall off to sleep eventually with sheer exhaustion and so lay on the settee as she had done the day before and let her mind take over. It felt like a knotted ball of wool, snatches of her life since she had known Andrew, and the outcome of it all, running through her head in a non-sequence of events, good and bad. When the latter came, floating up in her conscience the sadness and the futility of it all hit her hard and she broke down again in uncontrollable sobbing. Bob and Jill just left her to cry her grief and anger out of her system as far as that was possible. There was nothing they could do, but respect her privacy. They stayed nearby to give her their support when she pleaded for it with her wet, red eyes.

Bob got up from his armchair, walked across to the settee, and stroked her hair as she passed through to the hall and on to his study. Jill stayed in the kitchen and arranged some lunch, with little enthusiasm. He closed his study door very quietly. He usually left it slightly ajar so that Jill did not feel completely cut off from him, and he liked to hear her moving about the house. He took the crumpled envelope out of his pocket and slit the top with his bone handled letter opener. He put aside Andrew's letter, which was folded in an official brown envelope inside one from the Governor of the Prison, and read the information which he had already been told by George Carruthers the day before. The letter ended with words of sympathy for Susan and all the family.

Bob then picked up Andrew's envelope and took out the letter, which had obviously been read and possibly photocopied for evidence at the inquiry to come. He tentatively unfolded it and read slowly,

Dear Susan,

Thank you for your letter that has left me more devastated than I was before. I had kept a little glimmer of hope, though not much, that you would find it in your heart to forgive me. What I did was inexcusable I know. I now realise that money isn't everything and too often the craving for it leads to ultimate unhappiness as it has with us both, and would have done to many others had I not been found out.

I did not mean to imply in my letter that you were partly to blame. I only wanted you to know that I wished to have a comfortable start to our lives together. I love you more than I can tell you and have no wish to go on with my life without you being a part of it.

You are completely exonerated from any blame, Darling Susan, and I want you to forgive me for all the unhappiness I am now causing you and your good family.

I hope with all my heart that you will eventually forget me and find someone more worthwhile than myself, to love and to cherish you as much as I have done ever since I met you.

Goodbye, my Darling Sue,

Andrew.

Bob re-read the letter twice while deciding what course of action to take. He then opened the bottom drawer of his desk, slipped the letter into a folder, and closed it again. He felt that Susan was in no fit state of mind to have her heart rent asunder more than it was and decided to show it to her at some point in the future when time had healed her wounds a little.

Jill came to his study door but seeing it closed came to the conclusion Bob was having a private cry to himself. She left him, returned to the kitchen after taking a peep at Susan on the drawing room settee, and was glad to find her fast asleep. Bob came out of his study, crept past Susan to the drinks cabinet and poured out a stiff whisky for himself and a gin and vermouth for Jill. He took them into the kitchen and quietly told Jill he had received the letter and hidden it away. She agreed with his decision and did not wish to read it herself.

'I shall be glad when Robert comes home this evening. He is quite philosophical and will help her to be more objective about the whole situation,' she said miserably. Bob put his arm around her shoulder and they drank to Susan and the good fact that they had discovered Andrew's weaknesses of character before the wedding date.

'Better to walk towards the horizon with your feet firmly on the ground than to reach for the sky,' he quoted the philosophy he had always taught his children.

'If only Andrew had been taught that' Jill said.

Epilogue

For many months after the ghastly traumas leading up to and including, above all, Andrew's suicide, Susan lived in a sombre state of unhappiness. She found difficulty in coming to terms with Andrew's despicable actions. She often had nightmares involving the boat, its destruction and Harry's death. She felt angry that he had encouraged Andrew to get involved in drug dealing, and at his weakness in doing so.

Susan was strong enough to resist forgiveness, but wished she had waited for a longer period before writing that letter to him which caused him to take his life. Despite this she could never have continued the relationship.

Bob and Jill tried to console her as much as possible and for a long time she lived at home with them, trying to hide her inner feeling of utter loss. She returned to her job and workmates, only after coming to terms with her situation enough to do so. Her nearest friends came to her new flat which she rented after realising she could no longer face living where Andrew and she had been so happy together.

For over two years Susan wished for no male relationship, but eventually met David Bond to whom she related her past traumas at a Costa coffee house she frequented. Part of her broken heart had healed and she began to feel the inner joys of happiness again, much to her parents' delight.

Susan and David were married three years after Andrew's death and had two children. To everyone's delight.